A Hint of Crime

The second anthology from The Bristol

Fiction Writers' Group

Published by Snub Try Publishing

Copyright 2015 The Bristol Fiction Writers' Group

ISBN 978-0-9956728-0-2

Dedicated to the memory of:

Elizabeth 'Liz' Ann Ascott

Artist, writer, fabulous eccentric.

Eileen Elsey aka D A Allen

An elegant writer, both in prose and presence.

Contents

The Cuckoo and the Phoenix

A A Abbott

He'd always loved to go home. The night before the funeral,
he slept in his old bed. Crisp sheets, smelling of Daz, always
made up for him in the little bedroom. Old Eagle annuals,
temptingly shiny on the tall bookshelves. The familiar rustle of
oak trees at the window. Although his father had renounced
smoking and spent the last year of his life close to an oxygen
cylinder, the house still smelled of the sweet pipe tobacco the
old man had favoured. His own property somehow reeked
faintly of drains and stale curry, evidence of a man living alone
and working long hours.

His parents had been the one constant in his life. In London,
jobs, friends, relationships, even flats, came and went.
Landlords sold up, companies were taken over, friends moved
away.

There were a surprising number of people at the funeral, a
hundred at least. Beneath the bald spots and wrinkles, he
recognised several old school friends, now middle aged:
Johnny, who went into the police force; Terry, who worked on
the buses; Amanda – who knew what Amanda did? Once he
would have cared a great deal, but no longer. The years had

not been kind to them. Looking at their faces, he realised they thought the same of him. Ruefully, he fingered his thinning hair. They invited him for a drink afterwards at the Hare on the Hill. It had been the Mason's Arms, rough as a pit-bull, in his youth. Now it was everything he thought a pub should be: light, wooden floored, smoke-free, serving well-kept beer.

"Prices are on the high side, mind," Terry warned.

"They're worse in London," he said, almost enjoying Terry's scandalised expression.

"Will you move back now?" Amanda asked. "The house will be yours, I suppose." He noticed a hint of desperation in her eyes as she downed a dry white wine, her third within the hour.

"No, there's no going back," he said, a remark that covered all the bases, he thought. He added, "That house is ugly. Like a cuckoo in the nest. They wouldn't get permission to build it now."

It was a brown and white sixties monstrosity, put up cheaply on a bombsite, dwarfed by its grand Georgian neighbours. A good address though, in fact better than it was in the old days. Young professionals had realised you could walk to the city centre in ten minutes. Now the street was home to doctors, lawyers and accountants. A teacher like his father could never afford it.

The house didn't sell. Every fortnight, he spent a weekend there, tending the garden. Lawns were mown, shrubs trimmed, weeds composted. Inside the house, he flicked a duster around occasionally, but it stayed remarkably clean now nobody lived there. When he slept, exhausted, in his old bed, he felt his father watching him approvingly. He painted the front door to give the property kerb appeal, to leap up and grab the hearts of buyers.

He took to visiting the Hare on Sunday evenings. Terry and Johnny, maybe both, usually wandered in and shared reminiscences over a pint.

"Schooldays, eh. Best days of your life," Terry said.

He was silent. He remembered his youth in Bristol as a time of boredom, frustrations, injustice. Caned by the headmaster for misdeeds that were not his. Sacked from the Jolly Boy pub for fiddling the till. He knew he'd never over or undercharged on purpose, and definitely hadn't stolen money. He suspected Amanda was the real culprit. Of course, he would no more have landed Amanda in trouble than cut off his right arm.

"Did you see the fire in the church hall two weeks ago?" Johnny asked, changing the subject. "You'd have been here then; it was a Saturday night."

"No."

"Shame. We're looking for witnesses. Not often we get cases of arson round here, now. I don't remember any for decades. There was quite a spate of it when we were young. Before you moved to London."

He looked into Johnny's eyes, sensing an agenda. There was nothing to see; Johnny was far too professional for that. "Better be off now. Up early tomorrow to go back to work." He drained his pint.

He took the milk train to London and fell asleep. His dreams were usually pleasant. This time, there was lighter fuel, paper, matches. The school; old Mr Barney's classroom and the headmaster's study. Delight as the flames took, staring at them, entranced, from their cubbyhole in the shrubs by the playground. Holding Amanda's hand at last. Horns, blue lights, voices, splashes. He awoke, ashamed, but chuckling to himself in spite of that. He had done more than hold Amanda's hand. They had kissed for the first time. Then, eyes sparkling, she had encouraged him to go further. He was oblivious to the busy firemen just feet away, and they to him. He was in love.

He drifted back to sleep, thinking of the wild look in Amanda's eyes, that look that always made him go weak at the knees. The dream was darker now. It was the Jolly Boy pub, silent and empty. Amanda had said so, and he thought so too until the fire took hold and they heard the screams. At once, the scene flicked to the local newspaper. Headlines mentioned the tramp in the basement. He woke with a start.

That never happened, he thought. Tramp. That was a word you didn't hear any more. There were travellers, who had lorries. There were the homeless, sitting in shop doorways wrapped in blankets, asking for spare change. When he first came to London, he had been surprised by the beggars in the streets of the richest city in one of the richest countries in the world. Tramps never begged. He recollected his father pointing one out to him on a drive through the countryside to collect birds' eggs, a boyhood passion he regretted in these more enlightened times.

"I've seen that fellow every year," his father said. "He works on the farms and moves on. He's been doing it since the war."

Why should the war have turned a man into a tramp? he had wondered. We won it, didn't we? Every week, he bought comics reliving highlights of the war; brave Tommies triumphing over stupid Jerries. Sometimes, for a change, we outsmarted the cunning Nips.

He couldn't imagine the tramp, young, lantern-jawed and brave, stepping into his comic strip and fighting for the Allies. The man was a collection of wrinkles and long whiskers, battered hat, torn clothes, walking through the hedgerows. Tramp, tramp, tramp. He tipped his hat as the car went by.

A car was no longer the badge of affluence it had once been. Everyone in Bristol seemed to have one, even the students who had a purpose-built colony nearby, new flats with underground parking. Even Amanda, who turned up in an old banger at the Hare one Sunday evening, and had to be persuaded to leave it there overnight.

"You've drunk a bottle of wine," he said.

"I'll have to stay with you then," she told him.

He tried not to recoil. That wild look was upon her again, except now he saw it for what it was; a kind of madness. That would have been enough to deter him, but there was more: the grey roots of her bleached blonde hair, her face a mass of smoker's wrinkles, her once lithe body run to fat. She had changed, and he had too; he had escaped his childhood, risen like a phoenix from its ashes.

Terry broke the awkward silence, offering to run her back. Johnny raised an eyebrow, but they knew Terry had nursed a single pint all night; he was on an early shift the next morning.

After a couple of months, he knocked £20,000 off the price. Miracle of miracles, a buyer emerged.

Although he had exchanged contracts now and he could have let the weeds grow, he returned one more time to do the garden. It would be his last farewell to his father, to his roots. All week, the weather in London had been hot and humid.

Arriving in Bristol, he knew a storm was about to break. Dark clouds bore down on the city. He quickly took out the lawnmower, spade and shears, and set to work. When the first heavy drops fell, he had to rush to replace the tools in the shed.

Then an electrical storm began. The air around him trembled as lightning crackled, thunder following just a second or so later. He knew it meant that electricity was close. There were massive trees in the garden: an old oak, an outsize holly bush, a sycamore that dwarfed the house, all planted or self-seeded in the days of Queen Victoria. A bolt could strike them at any moment; he must stay inside the shed, breathing in the scent of pipe tobacco that still clung to the tiny wooden structure.

Thunder filled his ears, deafening him, the sound of a cross god shouting, of his father chiding him for selling and moving away. He watched with fascination as lightning flashed across the roof of the ugly squat house, not once, but twice, three times.

The storm moved on, taking with it the rainclouds that could have saved the building. Flames began to take hold. Then, as he heard an enormous bang, louder than the thunder, he remembered the oxygen cylinder in the living room. There was no saving the cuckoo now.

He stared into the fire, grinning, mesmerised, even when his landscape was filled with sirens and blue lights and Johnny was nudging his elbow.

Flight 6051

D A Allen

Everyone is rushing to get into the queue at the airport departure gate. The line doubles back on itself twice so that the crowd can fit into the confined space. They drag behind them a motley collection of wheeled trolleys – some expensive, some battered, some rather lacking in good taste:

there seems to be a penchant for fake leopard-skin and neon this year.

Unlike the old days, it is usually impossible to judge how affluent passengers are by their luggage, as if the more wealthy are scared of looking as if they have money. That oasis of privilege the Executive Lounge is now populated by people whose employers have given them a pass, rather than true First Class travellers. Few people dress properly for the journey either; they favour comfort over giving a smart impression and usually have recourse to sportswear. If everyone who wore "jogging bottoms" actually jogged, there would be an end to the nation's obesity problem.

Personally, I am most punctilious about my clothing. I have a variety of well-cut, dark suits. They are smart but unobtrusive. I like a capacious inside breast pocket, and it takes a good tailor to cut a jacket that hangs well over its contents. Apart from businessmen and women on domestic flights, however, suits are becoming the exception amongst air travellers. The days when even economy class travellers would dress smartly in the hope of being upgraded are over, as budget airlines rarely have anything to be upgraded to. This all makes my job more difficult, but I enjoy the challenge.

As usual, people prefer to stand rather than take a seat – herded into a line in a hot, airless space for half an hour or more; before the plane they will depart on has even arrived. They seem to disbelieve the boarding card they hold in their hand (or, perhaps, have on their phone) with its clearly stated seat number. Even ones with young children, now getting fractious after an early start and a long journey to the airport, stand surrounded with the paraphernalia which parenthood seems to require these days.

Most of the chairs are empty, but I scan the ones that are taken. A tanned woman – Spanish, I think, and in her 30s – is using her neon orange luggage as an impromptu table to consume a bread and chorizo snack. She wears gold hoop earrings, but they are thin and probably gilt. The only other jewellery she wears is an engagement ring, and I surmise that her picnic means that she cannot afford to eat in a café.

Near her sits a businessman intent on his iPad, also Spanish, judging by his well-cut lightweight suit. (Englishmen rarely spend enough money on a summer suit, so that they either hang badly, or wrinkle, or both.) He is handsome and assured, two qualities I may either resent or admire in a person, depending on my mood. Today, I am veering towards resentment. Now that aircraft seats are assigned in advance, I have little time to plan and act, and I don't think this one is suitable. He is wearing no jewellery whatsoever, and – rather than an expensive leather briefcase – he has a lightweight laptop bag. His shoes, too, have seen better days, and he appears to be worryingly young and fit. Perhaps his mother bought him the suit to help further his career.

One man sits perfectly relaxed, as if he is sitting in his own garden on a sunny day, and indeed he looks more like a gardener than an air passenger. His jumper is in danger of becoming completely unravelled by the end of his journey. The ribbing at the neck is almost detached from the body of the jumper – literally hanging by a thread – and there is a lengthy tail of wool drooping from the gaping hole beneath it. I find the disregard for appearance that the state of the garment proclaims profoundly shocking. His bag, propped against his leg like an over-affectionate pet, is also unusual – a narrow, khaki canvas sack with a bright red drawstring. It looks as if it once contained a bedroll. There's no carrying strap and he holds it by the gathered neck. I wonder for what destination or activity he thinks this is serviceable luggage. His footwear also draws my attention. He is wearing old, heavy leather lace-up boots made for long-distance walking or marching.

With no better quarry in view, I sit down next to him. I'm curious, if nothing else.

'You've decided not to queue, then?' I venture.

He shrugs, looking amused. 'We all have our plane seats already.'

He brushes back his grey hair – which needs the attentions of a good barber – to reveal blue eyes in a lined but smiling face.

I nod. 'It does seem rather unnecessary. Is that all you have with you?' I gesture towards the narrow sack.

'Oh yes. If I need anything else, I'll buy it.'

The conjunction of someone who dresses like a tramp but carries enough money to buy whatever he wants intrigues me.

'How true. I can tell you're a seasoned traveller.' A little bait to catch this fish.

'Yes, since I sold the business, I can go where I want when I want.'

'That must be such a change for you. What was the business?'

'Hoppers.'

'Pardon?'

'Space Hoppers. Those bright orange monstrosities that children sat and bounced around on.'

'I don't think I've ever…'

'No, I doubt if you have. But they were very popular at the time – made millions.'

'How extraordinary!'

'Yes, but then business started to decline, and I was worrying about my employees, and the management team were bickering on how to deal with it. I got fed up with it.'

'I can imagine.'

'So now I can do whatever I want. I'm off to Malaga to meet some friends.'

'It's a lovely city. You'll find much to see and do there.'

'Yes, I've never been before. My friends say there are some great bars around the port area.'

'There's also some excellent museums nowadays...'

I'm interrupted in listing the cultural attractions of Malaga by the public address system. A tinny voice with an atrocious Bristol accent announces that our flight is delayed.

My neighbour stands up. 'I'm going to the Gents if that's the case.' He brushes back his hair again, it's obviously a habitual gesture, and I notice that he is wearing a substantial gold ring with a beautiful, glinting diamond. Impressive.

He ambles away towards the toilet. I decide that this unusual mark is worth a try. I follow, my hand seeking the trusty black cord in my right jacket pocket as I do so.

He is standing at the washbasin as I come up behind him, moving swiftly. The cord is now ready, stretched between both hands. But as I raise it over his head, he turns, much quicker than I think possible. Somehow, he ducks past my

18

outstretched hands and slips behind me. One arm is round my neck, pressing hard. I try to shout, and manage a barely audible croak lost in the crackle of the public address system announcing that Flight 6051 is boarding. The cloying odour of mothballs fills my nostrils as I struggle, struggle to breath.

I collapse into unconsciousness as his other hand deftly reaches into my inside pocket and seizes the hoard of wallets there.

The Beast

Liz Ascott

It was a torpid Wednesday afternoon in late June. A day I will always remember. The year was 1958. I had decided to trundle round Hyde Park on one of those open-top sightseeing buses. The passengers on the upper deck appeared to be dozing. Resting my books on my lap, I began fanning myself with my copy of The Times. From time to time, the bus stopped, allowing people to depart and alight. And then it happened.

From out of nowhere a huge sand-coloured beast appeared, rearing up on its hind legs and circling the bus in a sloppy loose-limbed fashion. Some of the passengers on the upper-deck craned forward, mouths open – others remained seated in petrified friezes. In shape and colour the beast greatly resembled the lion family – though double the size of its captive cousins. The flattened sun-face framed by frills of ragged hair seemed to be searching our faces.

Down in the park, the animal's sudden appearance was causing havoc. People who minutes previously, had been sunning themselves on the parched turf, ran screaming in all directions – into fountains, public lavatories, shops and side-streets.

I should tell you, I am a rational man, an Academic – but all sorts of fantastical thoughts raced through my mind as I gazed down at those mournful eyes. I knew the beast had experienced centuries of animal and human misery. And I knew it was me the beast was seeking.

As suddenly as it had appeared the creature vanished, bounding off towards Piccadilly Circus. We passengers stumbled down the staircase to stand in the shade of the bus. A mother held her child tightly, kissed the top of its head.

Young men laughed nervously, mopped their faces, slicked back their greasy Teddy boy hairstyles. The driver and his conductor lit cigarettes and shook their heads in disbelief.

My intention of returning home, now seemed out of the question. A spell had been cast upon me. I set off at a trot, mindlessly crossing roads, narrowly missing a taxi as it pulled away from the pavement. Buying a packet of Marlboros (I never smoke) I paced to and fro outside a tobacconists, puffing and discarding cigarettes.

From the open doorway of an Expresso Bar came the thump, thump of that dreadful rock and roll rubbish on a juke box. A group of so-called teenagers had gathered on the pavement, hips swaying, fingers snapping, jumping and yelling in time to the beat. A girl in a red skirt span towards me, ponytail slicing the air, bright eyes holding mine at every turn. As she danced back to her spider-legged, rubber-soled companions she grinned and beckoned me. The driving rhythm made me feel quite faint. What the hell was going on? Not so long ago this country faced invasion. We didn't need more shake-ups.

I had to talk to someone. Joseph Hooper lived in Bloomsbury Square, just round the corner from the British Museum. He'd come up with a sane explanation.

As I approached the house, I wondered if Hooper had divined the true nature of my rather frequent visits. His younger sister, Margaret, might at that very moment be arranging flowers in the threadbare sitting room.

When I entered the flat, my pulse raced, for the air was perfumed with lilac. I tried to tell Hooper about the beast, but a lump rose in my throat, making speech impossible. Only after downing several glasses of water, was I able to describe what had happened.

'It wanted to communicate, Hooper,' I said. 'It wanted a response from me.' Hooper's ears reddened, his brow furrowed, his body stiffened with embarrassment. He shrugged dismissively.

By now tears were streaming down my face. Grabbing a drying-up cloth, which was lying on the table, I began dabbing at my eyes.

'Damn it, man. Haven't you got anything to say?'

I pointed at the lilacs in the glass vase, on the dresser.

'Margaret. She's here?'

I'd seen Margaret only a handful of times – but she possessed an indefinable quality. She hovered in my mind as she'd hovered in the flat.

'Well,' I said, picking up my books, 'I'll be off then.'

Still hoping for a crumb of encouragement I turned back at the door. Hooper inclined his head towards me, the thin line of his mouth lifting slightly. But he said nothing.

As I descended the stairs fetid smells of boiled food and perspiration rose to meet me. I could have sworn I heard a light footfall at my back. A foolish fancy, for I was alone.

To my surprise I found I was still clutching Hooper's drying-up cloth. Over the banister with you I thought, leaning forward to watch its progress. But what I saw falling through the column of stale air was a dark-haired young woman in a print frock; arms wide, half-smiling – cut-lilacs turning and falling round her. Moments later came the muffled thud of her body hitting the black and white tiles of the ground floor.

Down in the Communal Garden, opium poppies pushed their way through the iron railings, staining my trousers with their inky pollen. Pulling at a poppy head, I inhaled its musky fragrance, rubbed its gossamer petals between my fingers – before tossing it in the path of a bus. A splash of crimson on sticky black tarmac.

I felt I had entered a dream world, and longed to return. Checking the papers and listening to the News for sightings of the beast, provided an anchor, of sorts. Perhaps, when I'm idling on a bench, one sultry summer's day, the beast will jump from a parapet to rest its great head against my shoulder. I dream of such things. And the young girl capering about in the street? Nothing more than a wanton pleasure-seeker. A symptom of the unravelling of our Post-war times.

Margaret's presence however, pervades the dark interior of the Polish restaurant in which I dine, most evenings. A restaurant in which, like a coded message, the pungent scent of lilac hangs in the air. Only I see her ghostly fingers lift the pages of the menu on the wooden stand, topple the serviette cones on the tables. Soon she will drift out through the swinging door – into the suffocating embrace of night.

Moving House

Joe Beasant

The sound of crunching gravel on his driveway, under a car's wheels, brought Geoffrey back to the present. He stood up from the solitary chair, looked around the room, so clear and simple now, stripped of Janet's clutter and influence, an empty house ready for new residents. It had taken interminable bus trips to and from the local charity shops with bags of her clothes. The unwanted furniture, ornaments and accumulated nick nacks of a life-time, went to a local auction house. There was nothing left to remind him of the pain he'd endured.

People had been so shocked by her death, friends had endlessly given their commiserations and tried to show him support. They'd been childhood sweethearts, there had never been anybody else for either of them, they had got married at the earliest opportunity.

Their daughter had arrived the day after Janet's death, full of tears and questions, shocked and puzzled. She had stayed until soon after the funeral, helping him to sort out arrangements and her mother's clothes. She had left tearfully to return north to her job, insisting he kept in contact daily. Since then he'd put the house on the market, accepting an offer that exceeded the estate agents original estimate, enabling him to buy a spacious flat in a new housing development. It would be a fresh start for him in a different environment, bright and modern, minimalist and made for clear thought.

Leaving the room he shut the door, took one last look around the hallway, the polished wood floor, that Janet had always been so proud of, reflecting the silhouette of the figure outside, who had just knocked loudly on the obscured glass front door. It must be the taxi he thought. Picking up his suitcase he stepped forward into his new life, opening the door as the man raised his hand to knock again.

"Geoffrey Toohey? You are under arrest for the murder of Janet Toohey. You do not have to say anything…"

Flyleaf

Judy Darley

I only notice her initially because of the air of awkwardness she exudes. A flicker of fear, a twist of embarrassment and a bright spark of excitement. Like a child stealing candy, yet what she's doing... what is it that she's doing?

I watch her fluttering around Powell's City of Books, hesitating at certain shelves, peering at the lettered spines, opening her backpack, fishing out a book. She glances around furtively, guiltily, stuffs the book onto the shelf, and flits away. The reverse of stealing: surreptitious gifting?

I follow her at a distance, looking at the shelves she has been adding to, and find I can't tell which books she has inserted. It seems whichever volumes were retrieved from her bag have been placed in exactly the space for which they were intended.

Then I reach one where there was clearly no gap to fill, and see a book resting atop of the others, the same title and author, but not yet catalogued by Powell's – an outsider in their midst. I pick it up, rifle gently through its pages. I even raise it to my nose and quietly inhale, but it smells only of paper, of dust; pleasing smells.

The book itself is perhaps the only clue: Jack Kerouac's 'On The Road'. And scribbled onto the flyleaf: '*To Mara. Hope the journey is every bit as much of an adventure as the destination. Love N.*'

So now I have a name. The book is well-thumbed, presumably well-read, or possibly just worn out with being stuffed into the bottom of a backpack. But why abandon a book that evidently meant so much to her?

She's leaving the bookshop. I follow as fast as I can without visibly chasing her. I try to appear aloof, perhaps even a little self-obsessed, trying to maintain the persona I assumed on leaving the gym earlier this morning.

She stops off at the market, strolling through it slowly, fingering items of jewellery, ceramic dishes, metallic sculptures, as though trying to read a secret Braille imprinted just below the surface. She pores over a table of books, picking up several and putting them back, then selects one and buys it. I have a flash of understanding. Not only is this a woman on the move, possibly in the middle of the journey mentioned on the Kerouac flyleaf, but she's a woman who loves books. Devours them. She has to get rid of some to be able to carry and read more.

So smug am I at my deduction that I accidentally pass her right by without realising she's paused again, this time at a fruit stall where sleepy bees or wasps buzz around spilt juice. I halt behind a rail of vintage clothes that stink of basements and mothballs, and watch as she runs her palms over the furry scalps of a tray of peaches. She caresses their silken skin and chats to the stallholder. Her voice is clipped – British in that way that somehow rings of money, a thought possibly confirmed when she fills a paper bag with the fruit, pays for them, and then goes to a nearby wall where she sits and eats two in quick succession, quietly spilling over with a kind of greedy delight. The voraciousness with which she consumes them gives the impression, momentarily, of her tearing the peaches limb from limb, stuffing her mouth with their soft, sweet flesh so that the juice runs down her chin. I'm simultaneously repelled by and drawn to the sight, my own mouth filling with a vicarious flood of moisture.

She plops the peach stones into a trashcan, wipes her hands briskly on a serviette and tosses that in too, then continues on her journey. She walks in a way that emphasises her out-of-town-ness to me, taking an erratic route through the streets that seems to speak more of impulse than plan. I know too much about both of those feelings, and think to myself again of that night at the bar, that girl with her hair long and glossy, her seemingly sugar-dusted eyes. Her skin smelled of tequila and frangipani flowers. What I did to her in the alley was carefully planned, but only after giving in to an impulse.

This girl, Mara, gazes around herself hungrily as she walks, staring upwards into the blue Oregon sky as passing residents of the city stare only at their feet.

I follow her gaze and see the things I rarely notice, haven't paid attention to since I was a child visiting my uncle and aunt here. She spends a good few minutes looking up at Portlandia, the gigantic statue at Fifth Avenue. I remember my uncle schooling me on her, on how she's based on Portland's seal;

38 feet tall, made from 1,000 pounds of hammered copper sheets. A vast goddess of a woman.

Yet, since I arrived back in the city, this is the first time I've looked up and reacquainted myself with the wonder of this work of art.

Caught up as I am in this minor, one-sided reunion, that I almost miss Mara moving on again, striding purposefully this time, like something in the guidebook she's been flicking through has caught her eye. She marches towards the federal courthouse set between Salmon Street and Third Avenue. I almost stop in my tracks as she enters, almost drop the whole plan as a cold self-preserving fear shoots through me, but then I remember my suit, my freshly washed hair. Only my half-rotting sneakers could give me away. The gym-jock I lifted the clothes from had tiny shoes, like a woman's, though the suit hangs from my shoulders. I've gotten skinnier since leaving Seattle.

I observe through the glass of the doors, like I'm watching TV, as Mara chats with the security guard, hands over a camera, a cheap disposable one that wafts another wave of doubt over me. Maybe she's not the right target after all. This whole day could have been a waste of my energies.

Still, I automatically take note as she enters the elevator, of the numbers lighting up till she reaches Floor 9. I have to see this through now, don't I? My mom always taught me to see things through.

I've learnt a lot over the past few months: which soup kitchens will feed you best on which nights; how to slip into the gymnasium's changing rooms to sneak a few moments of hot water and steam. I don't normally steal anything, but who leaves a three-hundred dollar suit hanging from a hook when there are lockers available? Seems to me he was practically offering it up as a donation.

I left him my ratty old jeans as an exchange, which in my mind sets things right, at least a little.

At the ninth floor of the courthouse the elevator opens onto a garden. It catches me by surprise; sunshine sharp against my eyes, warm on my skin. Never knew it was up here. I stand still for a moment, taking in the greenery, the trickling water features, playful sculptures of bronze animals in a courtroom scenario – the city beyond, sleepy and quiet in the fall sunlight.

I spy Mara at last, sit beside her where she's filling a small notebook with scrawling text.

"What's that you're writing?" That's it, friendly, casual.

She smiles at me, seems unalarmed. "A travelogue. I've been travelling, right through California, now Oregon, then on to Seattle, maybe Vancouver too."

"Wow, that's some trip!" I say, thinking, she's going the opposite direction to me, going up as I go down.

She smiles at me and I catch a glint of her teeth, see her in my mind tearing into those peaches, juice running down her face. See myself tearing into her, her sweetness on my skin, my lips, my tongue. My breath quickens and I lean fractionally towards her, inhale. The smell of peaches fills my head.

My belly rumbles at the thought.

She's moving, but not away from me, reaching into her backpack again, her hand closing over something. A weapon? Do British girls carry weapons? And would they have let her bring it into a Federal building, if they made her leave a camera at the desk?

My mind is spinning with possibilities, spinning with hunger, so I can barely see what she's holding out to me: a gift, round and swollen. I blink, see her smile. I take the peach she offers me and hold it to my nose.

"Have it," she says, and her voice is kind in a way that makes me stumble inside. "They're good."

I open my mouth wide, and take a bite.

The Cleaner

J E Hagan

I'm the cleaner now, just like I was the cleaner before, but the management don't need to know that. I just smile, do my job, and go home.

Don't rich people have any imagination? Why anyone would think that having dinner in a disused police station is stylish is beyond me. But then again, Dario, the manager, knows how to make them cough up. From the minute they come through the polished double doors, with their old-fashioned blue lamps, into the bar with wanted posters (fake) and truncheons (real) on the wall, they are seduced.

The air is warm and smells of all things tasty, and it's generally the sound of the blues that comes out of the speakers, including what Dario now calls the 'Intimate' areas. Intimate, my Aunt Sally. They are windowless cells, pure and simple. They've still got the big doors with the locks, (but no keys; they're upstairs in the safe), and peepholes. One of them even has a two way mirror, very amusing ha, ha, yours for a negotiable price.

These rich blokes bring their birds in, all smelling of wine and waving their Pandora bracelets in the air, and eat a meal it would take me all week to earn. The birds tend to laugh a lot in these 'Intimate' rooms, get a bit scared, a bit excited, if you know what I mean.

Oh, if only they knew. Those nice birds should come down here in the day, when the music's off and the strip lights are on, and see if they notice the difference. There were people who died in those rooms. But of course they weren't 'rooms' then, they were cells, and although the paperwork may say 'natural causes', a heart attack can be brought on by many things.

But as I said at the start, I'm just the cleaner, and I keep what I know to myself. So, what happened? Mines a pint – with a whisky chaser. Ta. Well, it was a few years ago, just after the July bombings. This chap Clive was brought into the station. Big bloke, a cabby, stunk of fags. Want to know who ate all the pies? It was Clive. Generally had a bag of doughnuts or something on the dashboard.

Well, some silly bint rang in complaining that he'd touched her up. She'd sat in the front seat, dropped her handbag on the floor, and she reckoned Clive groped her boob helping her find her purse. Couldn't find it. According to her, Clive says, thinking she never had a purse in the first place, and was after a freebie.

'Never mind, I'll give you a ride if you give me one' – there's girls round here who pay for their lifts in trade, if you get me.

Anyway, the stupid tart wasn't having it. She called the boys in, and that's when the real trouble started. They found the purse alright, but they also found a gun. Oh, dear.

So a couple of the boys took old Clive downstairs, to one of the posh 'rooms' only back then it just had a table and two chairs, all bolted to the floor, a light bulb with a cage round it, and a smell of bleach to cover the other smells. A detective and a uniform, a sergeant, came in, and put a tape recorder and stuff on the table. Clive tried to be friendly and smile, but the sarg wouldn't smile back – must be the special training. In the pub he'd be Jack the Lad, but put him in front of a crim, even someone he knew, and he might as well be a statue. Old Clive was already so nervous he was trumping like a Sally Army band, which didn't help in a room like that.

The detective didn't like Clive anyway; he had a grudge against him. Clive might have been many things, but, give him his due, he never drove when he'd had a drink. Anyway, one night, this chap, no, I'm not telling you who, but I'm sure you can guess, needed to go somewhere in hurry, saw Clive in the pub and demanded a ride, and Clive refused. Not used to being told 'no' to, this bloke. Like I said, he had a grudge.

The DI sat down at the table, and pointed to the other chair. Clive squeezed in, breathing hard, the sharp edge of the table cutting into his belly.

'Just a few questions' the DI started. The usual, name, address, etcetera, as if he didn't know already.

'So, where did the gun come from?'

'I don't know.' Clive didn't know. He wasn't the type to make friends with blokes with guns. He worried too much and gossiped like a granny. He was already shiny with sweat, and it made a mess of his t-shirt and hair, and the BO just added to the fug.

'Don't lie to us. You don't just leave a gun in a cab. Someone left it there on purpose. Who?'

'I don't know, honest. I need to stand up, I can't breathe.' The DI knew that Clive didn't know, but he wanted to have a bit of fun with him.

'God you're a mess. Get up then. Some exercise should do you good, get you to think straight. Stretch out your arms, bend your knees. Go on, do it now. That's it, and again. Did I tell you to stop? Keep going until I tell you.' The sarg by the wall stared straight ahead and said nowt.

'Remember where the gun came from yet?' Clive shook his head, trembling all over, and wheezing something rotten.

'Okay, stop. Why don't you just jog round the room until you remember.' Clive held onto the table and struggled to breathe.

'I don't know where it came from. I've had a busy night. Anybody could have dropped it.'

'It wasn't just anybody though, was it? Come on, run.' So Clive ran, slowly, round and round the table, shoulders heaving, belly bouncing like a balloon full of water, and the bastard by the wall just watched.

After a while Clive fell down like a sack of spuds off a shelf and didn't move. He didn't so much as squeak.

'Get up, you slob' said the DI, but Clive didn't move. The DI gave him a sharp kick, but still no movement. The sarg checked his wrist, but no pulse. He called an ambulance, but Clive was dead before he reached the hospital, but not before the sarg was promised a promotion. The official verdict was that the prisoner, a grossly overweight man, a smoker who consumed alcohol regularly, had had a fatal heart attack.

It would be nice to say that the bastards who killed him got theirs, and that's why this place was closed, but it wouldn't be true. It closed because it was it was an old building and cost too much to repair. No poetic justice at all. And be on your best behaviour if you're ever over Canterbury way. Those two are still out there having fun.

Thanks for the drink, but I'd best be off now, I've got work to do.

The Convenience Store

Richard M S Kemp

"Hello, Ma?"

The sound of a great 18-wheeler rushes past my ears. It sends a shiver down the hairs on my back and rattles the glass around the payphone. I'm outside a lonely gas station on the side of the highway. It's hot as hell – even the lizards have gone into hiding. Me, I'm done hiding. I'm done running, too. They'll be with me soon enough. Just time to call my ole lady and say goodbye.

"Hello, Ma?"

I hear a rough voice crackle on the other end, but another 18-wheeler rolls by, shaking the coins inside the telephone and loosening two pictures of call girls from their greasy frames.

"Hello?"

I holler back this time. "Ma? Ma? It's Charlie!"

"What?" She sounds irritated. Probably already started drinking. Doesn't take long these days.

"It's Charlie, Ma. Your son."

"Oh…Charlie. What you callin' here for?" I hear the crack and hiss of a beer bottle being opened.

Sirens are wailing in the distance. They can't be far away now. Better make it quick.

***

Things were always gonna end up like this, I guess. Teachers knew it. Bosses knew it. Daddy definitely knew it — probably why he left. My high school yearbook had me down as the one 'most likely to be seen on that TV show *Cops*'. My brothers and sisters, they all disowned me — then they left for good, off to New York City to chase their dreams or some shit. They couldn't wait to get out. Ma was pretty much all I had left, but then her health started failing. She couldn't work no more and so it was down to me to earn the bread. Harder than it sounded, I tell you.

The clean route: I tried it, I really did. I got jobs as dishwashers, as porters, as gas station attendants, but nothing ever worked out, probably on account of how I would manage to fuck things up each time; sneaking the odd five out of the cash register or talking back to customers – I didn't have a smart mouth so much as a particularly stupid one.

One night, I came home to the trailer so exhausted I could barely speak. I saw Ma asleep, all shrivelled up in her wicker chair. The yellow-stained walls bore down on her, the stench of cigarettes and booze congealing in the thick night air. I was rolling from job to job, never making enough, and wondering why the hell I shouldn't just rob a bank or something. This was no life for nobody.

In the end, of course, the decision was made for me. I'd got fired from so many different places that pretty much everyone saw my resume coming from a mile away. The choice was either move towns or get one of them regular jobs. Not so easy when you flunk high school with zero qualifications – sales managers just don't seem to be hiring all of a sudden. Ma wasn't going any place anyhow; she'd raised her whole family in this town and grew up here herself. Plus, her health had gotten worse still – she was coughing and heaving and turning to the bottle more regular, figured she'd try self-medicating. I just couldn't keep up with all the expenses.

I don't know. Something happens to you out here, out in the heat. You find any way you can to keep your head above water. It started with some petty thefts – nothing major, a tankful of gasoline here, some illegal merchandise there. Eventually, though, I was leaving the trailer most nights, telling Ma how I was doing another night shift.

I got caught soon enough; I'd broken into a grocery store at night not realising the workers would be there restocking shelves. Cops went to Ma first and nabbed me when I arrived. That should've been the end of it.

Ma posted bail for me and so I promised to quit, but I couldn't. We needed the money and there wasn't a gas station or kitchen in town that would even consider hiring someone like me. I fell straight back in and, this time, I got caught quick.

Jail time's a bitch, the kind that follows you the rest of your life. I was in the penitentiary sixteen months in total and every day I thought about Ma, about what I'd done and how stupid it all was. By the time I got out, my name was all over town. Everyone knew who Charlie was – the fuckup of the family, the token trailer-park criminal.

I tried to get clean, even if Ma couldn't; she was drinking heavier than ever. One of the officers at the county jail helped me find a job as a kitchen porter. There was even the possibility of promotion to hygiene manager one day. But then,

Larry came along. Larry was an ole school friend I hadn't seen since we both failed to graduate. He'd come back after being kicked out by his ole lady. We were both poor as shit and with nothing to show for it. Larry had the idea of holding up a few places just outside town, to make some cash "and help us get back on our feet," he said. I figured 'what the hell?' and just went along with it. That was my first mistake.

Larry and I went on a spree of robberies in the area: restaurants, gas stations, you name it. We probably hit around five different places in a matter of weeks, one every other night. There was enough money now that we could call it quits, but Larry set his sights on this convenience store. It was a little out of the way, pretty much nothing but desert and silence, but there was loads of booze and so the cash prize could have been huge.

The air was dense with heat, like wading through soup. We parked up around noon; figured we'd try a day hit, change up the timings in case anyone had noticed a pattern. We'd gotten ourselves a couple pistols and burst through the rickety-ass door like we were a pair of ole West gunslingers or some shit. I spotted one other customer as we came through. He had his head in one of the fridges looking at the dairy. The storeowner, an ole weathered Mexican standing behind the register, he clocked us right away. "Larry?" he said, his thick Mexican accent rolling the two rs in his name.

"Oh shit," Larry said. I looked at him and saw the colour drain from his face.

I never intended on using the pistol; just wanted it for protection, really – to put the fear of God up people. Too bad, then, that the ole bastard had a double-barrelled shotgun tucked below the counter. He pulled it up and started firing. Larry scurried for a place to hide while I slid behind one of the deep freezers. The sound of each blast was like a steamroller going over my eardrums. I checked my pistol; the storeowner was unloading a couple more rounds, hitting everything in sight.

The noise stopped and the fridge guy made a run for it, probably thinking the ole man was on the reload, but he caught him in the chest before he even reached the door. Larry moved behind the potato chips and poked his head out to get a good shot, but he couldn't aim quick enough. He was dead in seconds.

I leaned against the back of the freezer. My heart was jacked up into the top of my throat, beating so loud I could hear an echo. It was just me and the ole man now and one of us was scared shitless. Still, I had to wonder why the storeowner knew Larry's name but not mine. Had he hit this place before?

News travels fast, even in a Podunk desert town like this. Either way, it was clear I was now part of this, too. I tried to take smaller breaths so as not to make much noise. I hadn't taken even a single shot, but my finger was shaking on the trigger. Sweat was sliding from my forehead into my eyes. The salt started to sting, but I didn't dare move to wipe it off.

The store filled with the smell of spent gunpowder – that and all the booze the ole Mexican had managed to hit. I could see Larry lying on the linoleum floor, his face frozen and staring right at me. Blood crept from underneath him, soaking his flannel shirt. The fridge guy I couldn't see anymore, though I had a feeling he was on the other side of my freezer.

I could hear the storeowner in the back, talking on a telephone. "…yes," he said, somehow calm. "Larry Giles, yes… and one more… yes. Thank you."

That was his full name, Larry Giles. The storeowner definitely knew him. 'And one more', though? The ole man must have figured he'd shot everyone. Not me. He'd forgotten about Charlie. I hung tight, my mind racing on what to do as my buddy's blood seeped closer towards me. I planned it out: I'd wait until the ole man was out of earshot and then run out the door faster than a jackrabbit, leap into the pickup and scream on outta there. Not much of a plan, I know, but it was the best I could come up with in the time I had. Didn't matter, though, as the ole man stalked towards me to check the bodies. He got right up to the deep freezer and then saw me hiding there. "¿Qué pinche...?" he started, but stopped short on account of me pulling the trigger and firing a shot right between his eyes. The explosion hammered my whole body backwards. I dropped the gun and shook off my hand.

I popped up, closing my eyes for a moment to let the blood rush back to my head, then strode over to the rickety ole door and pushed it open. It gave in with a squeak, as pure white light rushed in, blinding me. I searched for the pickup, slipped inside, started her up and headed out on the highway.

It didn't take long for the realisation to hit: I'd left my pistol behind the freezer. Plus, the guy had given Larry's name. Chances were that other people knew it too, cops especially. They were bound to find the ole Mexican lying there, see Larry and quickly count up to me. Then there were the fingerprints, security cameras. Nobody opens a convenience store on the outskirts of town, on a desert highway, without installing a half-decent surveillance system. I was fucked.

I drove as fast as I could, as far as I could, but it was never gonna work.

***

"Ma, you still there?"

"Yes, I'm still here, Charlie. Where else do you think I'd be? Where the hell are you?" I shudder at the sound of another bottle being squeezed open.

"I'm at a payphone, Ma."

"Payphone? What you doin' at a damned payphone for?"

"I'm tryin' to tell you, Ma!" I hold my palm over the receiver and take a deep breath. No use losing my temper now. "I messed up. Real bad this time."

I could hear Ma's wheezing getting louder. That was her rage filling up. "Charlie, you know I can't pay for no more bail. This time, you're on your own."

"That's just it, Ma. I ain't gettin' out this time."

The sirens are roaring now. It won't be long before they reach me. I'd run out of quarters anyway. I raise my voice above the din of police cars and 18-wheelers. I can hear cursing under Ma's breath.

"Ma, all's I wanna say is I love you." I feel a lump in my throat, my voice thinning. "And I'm sorry." I can barely get out that last part.

"Me too, Charlie," says Ma, curt as ever, and slams down the receiver.

I feel a rumble and then hear a grunt behind me. I turn to see the county sheriff, armed to the teeth and smiling big and wide. His huge glasses glint in the sunlight. He's red-faced, but not from sunburn. I drop the receiver, put my hands on my head, and say, "let's go."

Snip

Tim Kindberg

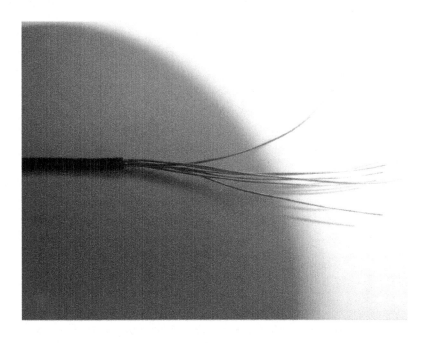

The snipping began in the summer, during a stretch of long and unusually hot days in the Bristol suburbs. Early one Saturday evening I opened all the doors and windows in the conservatory of our tidy home, and selected Bach's violin concerto in A minor. I closed my eyes, lay back in anticipation as the needle tracked the beginning of the disc's spiral groove. Before the music began, I just had time to think about how perfectly arranged my life had become with my new wife

Louise, who bent to almost my every whim. Life was perfect, that is, apart from her tyke of a teenage son, Nathan.

The first notes soared. But my senses were jarred as I quickly realised there was no sound emerging from the right-hand speaker. I stood up to confirm the disappointing truth, bending my ear to first one speaker then the other. Fortunately, I am a practical, rational man: too rational I have been told. But it has served me well in the Department. No fuss. No fuzzy intuition. Above all no superstition. Everything has a reason, a cause; a cause that can be divined via logical inference. Of mysteries, true mysteries, there were none.

I swopped the cables between the speakers. This time only the right-hand speaker sounded, which had been silent before, so that was not faulty. I turned my attention to the rest of my hi-fi system, which consisted of separate components neatly stacked on a small table. I switched the amplifier to take its source from the CD player instead of the record player. The same speaker was silent. My irritation at having to forgo Bach's sweetness began to be replaced by satisfaction with my deductive powers: the fault lay not with the deck, either, but with the amplifier.

A few days later, when I collected the amplifier from the repair shop, the rather cocky young man behind the counter smiled – disingenuously, I thought – as he informed me that no fault had been found. However they had checked and reseated the components within the amplifier. Perhaps either that or movement along the journey to the shop had fixed what was merely a loose connection.

However, when I reconnected the amplifier on returning home, the violin was once again absent from the same speaker. I went through all the checks I had performed before and reached the same conclusion.

It was while I was on the phone to the repair shop, arranging for them to have a proper look at the faulty amplifier this time, that I bent to look at the source cables connecting the stacked components, one from each of the record deck and the CD player to the amplifier. Each source cable consisted of two wires bonded together, one for each channel. I had had no reason to check these cables, which hung neatly and freely above the floor.

However, on close inspection, I saw that the right-hand channel's wire in each cable had been neatly cut. I quickly made an excuse and rang off.

I say 'cut' advisedly. Louise tried to persuade me that a rodent must have gnawed the wires but I was having none of it. I showed her, despite her protestations, the two clean snips. Moreover, the rodent would have had to climb and bite the cables more than a foot from the floor.

If there is one thing I regret about marrying Louise – apart from her tendency not to acquaint herself with facts, that is – it is Nathan, my stepson. He is a most resentful boy who fails to see the sacrifices I made when I took him, along with his mother, into my life.

I made quite a show of repairing the cables, one of whose replacements had to be soldered back into the innards of the record deck, a time-consuming process. I first brought the whole hi-fi system onto the table in the centre of the conservatory for a thorough examination. I wanted Nathan to see that I was not to be beaten. I also chose to make the repairs while my brother-in-law's family were visiting. For they, with their rather mischievous daughter Helena, had been our only visitors since I had last listened to my music.

I had two suspects. Each had the opportunity, for the conservatory was frequently unoccupied. Each had a motive: Nathan never bothered to hide his resentment towards me, and my seven-year-old niece showed a general propensity for trouble-making. But I could prove nothing. My resentment grew inside at whichever of them had targeted me specifically – for it was emphatically my hi-fi system; no one else used it.

On the other hand, I had to admit, if only to myself, that I could imagine neither of them having the dexterity or knowledge required to eliminate precisely the right-hand channel from each of the two cables. But what else was I to think? It could hardly be my new wife who had committed such an unreasoning, spiteful act.

It was some weeks later, when I had another cause for complaint about Nathan – they weren't exactly rare – that I found myself accusing him of cutting the cables. The boy was prone to naked audacity at the best of times. Not only did he deny it dismissively but he laughed in my face as he did so. To make matters worse, Louise took his side. She always does. No matter how egregious his lack of respect for me, she accuses me of being over-bearing towards him. Me!

I patiently explained that I had not sabotaged my own record player and that I would like to think she had not done so, either. Moreover, ghosts did not exist. If Nathan was not the culprit, in other words, then it must be young Helena. Louise began to cry. "How could you?" she exclaimed. "How could you accuse anyone in my family?"

I sighed, deeply. When it came to the crunch, I was the outsider in my own home. It did no good for me to appeal to the facts. However much it pained me, there was nothing to do but let the matter lie.

Until, that is, the snipping occurred again; this time without subtlety. One cable was cut clean through, the other lacerated. There was contempt in those cuts; in their malicious incision into my listening pleasure. Of course, I wasted no time in having it out with them. It was either Nathan or Helena, I repeated: she of the impish countenance who had recently visited us and enjoyed our sweets and hospitality. But Nathan's denial was even more scathing; his expression still more mocking. And his mother's distress, beyond the bounds of sense, at my accusations was pathetic. I threw my arms into the air and stormed out.

Much as I would like to control every aspect of our household, it simply was not practical to remove all sharp implements – the scissors and the knives in the kitchen, in the office upstairs, the garage and heaven knew where else. I had to inure myself to continuing vulnerability.

Incredibly, a week later, again it happened; the cable cut clean, after all the time, effort and money I had already spent on repairs. This time, I did not give them the satisfaction of a confrontation and instead issued a command. There was only one thing for it. They had to go. They had to leave my house.

I drove my wife and stepson to her brother's home. Let them stay there and stew. Let them fester in their guilty, unjust criticisms of my perfectly reasonable accusations. I no longer cared which young person was the perpetrator. I saw only that I, the victim, had been painted as a bullying villain; that I, who stood by reason and who wanted only to enjoy Bach in peace, had been horribly maligned by my so-called family. I almost – almost – wanted my first wife Mary back. As if that malignant personage could ever make me happy.

And so I spent months alone in the house, my time there untrammelled by impudence and whining. My phone rang but I did not answer. I set it to silent mode. My intact cables sweetly carried electrons to and fro, issuing Bach's blissful violins into my conservatory.

Until one cold night. I returned from the Department after a stressful day and took a mug of tea into the office upstairs to answer urgent emails, looking forward to the calming music I would listen to while I worked.

But one of the small speakers connected to the computer was mute. I found the cable snipped quite through. A doubt crept into my mind because this was the computer Nathan used for his homework while he listened to vile R&B or whatever the youth call their music nowadays. Had he been back to the house? But why would he damage something that would hurt him when – if – he ever came back to live here? Was this a bizarre way of clearing his name?

Of course, I had to change the locks. This incursion was unconscionable.

The days grew shorter. Then Christmas arrived. I was so caught up with my new-found isolation, living alone without disturbance, my belongings arranged just as I wanted them without compromise, perturbed only by the occasional twinge of remorse that I had been so harshly compelled to banish my new family, that I barely noticed Christmas coming. When I finally noticed the neighbours' lights around my house, I decided to buy a tree for the conservatory. I also bought the finest, brightest cherry-red lights to decorate it. And I sat admiring my tree while Bach's cool beauty filled the room. For several nights, after hard days in the Department, I returned to this sanctuary.

On Christmas Eve we were granted the afternoon off. I spent the free hours shopping and wrapping presents for myself – for I and my new family were completely estranged from one another by now. I laid my gifts beneath the tree and switched on the lights. Which remained unlit. I switched on the record player. There was no sound. All had been cut.

The windows downstairs showed no sign of breakage or entry. I walked through the silent hall and opened the front door. There was no sign of anyone outside, just the windows around me bright with Christmas tree lights.

Suddenly, behind me, music began playing from the computer upstairs, the music Nathan liked to listen to.

I went to the kitchen, took out a large pair of scissors from the drawer, and ascended the staircase.

Out of the Blue

Nigel Lapworth

This was it. It had to be. The site he'd been searching for for the past three months since his first tentative steps onto the dark web. It seemed perfect. He kicked student detritus under the sofa as he headed for the kitchenette in search of a Hershey bar and another can of lager to celebrate, his mind a maelstrom of dark thoughts and bright ideas. He scarcely noticed the dirty coffee cups, plates and assorted kitchenalia waiting patiently in the sink. He didn't even register that the ceiling light cluster was down to a single dingy bulb, or the worrying smell emanating from behind the fridge. All that mattered now was getting down to business and registering.

He'd decided years ago what pseudonym to use if, or indeed when the time ever came, but as he sat down in front of his tired pc to start his big adventure he had to wipe sweat from his palms. It all came down to this.

'Welcome to Blue Sky. Name?*'

Here goes nothing 'Moriarty'.

The cursor was flashing longer than necessary and his heart raced. 'We're sorry, Moriarty is already taken. Name?*'

Shit, shit, shit, shit, shit!

'Moriarty-007'

'Welcome to Blue Sky Moriarty-007. Please enter a valid email address*'.

Five minutes later Patrick Horstairs from Dagenham was a fully-fledged member of the Blue Sky club. He'd had to give real details about himself of course, but he still couldn't believe it. At last! A great wave of relief flooded every nerve ending, yet he found he didn't quite know what to do with himself now. The website had promised email confirmation once his application had been verified, but that would take at least twenty four hours. That meant there had to be a real person somewhere carrying out real checks on him. Wow! They wouldn't find anything of course because there was nothing to find – no criminal record, no shoddy credit history, not so much as an unpaid parking ticket. He was clean. He *had* to be an ideal club member.

He wandered back to the kitchenette and started doing the washing up. A street light was shining through the single window. It must be gone three by now he thought. He could see his reflection in the grimy glass and studied his face. He wished his bum-fluff would sort itself into a beard, and he'd have to tidy himself up a bit before he met his crime team, but other than that he was just another ordinary young student of no particular note. He smiled to himself. That's just the way it should be. A perfect disguise.

The Dog and Rocket was a bustling, boozy kind of place where the locals managed to rub along with strangers provided they all pushed off before nine o'clock and didn't empty the fruit machine. It was close to a Tube Station and found a willing clientele working in the nearby offices that nipped in for a pint or two after work before heading home, and just as often by couples meeting on the sly. It had taken Patrick twenty minutes to get there on his bike which was chained, securely he hoped, to a lamp post outside.

He'd managed to find a seat at a table with his back to the wall, from which he could survey both the bar and the door — and been well pleased with himself until he'd had to nip for a piss and came back to find two old grumps sitting at his table playing dominoes. One of them owned a terrier that sat by his feet, its evil face apparently set in a permanent snarl. Patrick had dragged his rucksack and bike helmet out from under the table lest the sly beast start humping them, or some such. He was now wedged uncomfortably between one of the old grumps and the wooden end of a window seat, his rucksack and helmet on his lap and nowhere to put his pint down. Worse still, while he could still see some of the bar, his view of the door was almost non-existent.

He gave up and went to get a refill.

It was as he was draining his glass that he heard a gruff voice further down the bar asking for a bottle of Blue Sky. He froze for a second. That *had* to be the contact! There were too many people in the way and he couldn't see the person who'd ordered the drink, but he watched in fascination as the barman turned to a fridge at knee level and retrieved what appeared to be a bottle of foreign beer. He didn't see where the customer went after paying for his drink, but he figured he'd be able to find him; after all, how many people in this pub would be drinking a foreign beer no one had ever heard of?

He knew exactly what to order and, having hoisted his rucksack, his bike helmet firmly attached to it by its strap, made his way through the crowds to find the man with the matching bottle.

It didn't take him long. He was a short, square-shaped brute of around thirty with a flattened, bristly face and an incongruously long nose. He was sitting in a booth across from a taller, thinner man who appeared older and more carefully groomed. They both sat back in their seats as Patrick approached as though they'd been talking. The taller man nodded at Patrick's bottle, smiled briefly and indicated with a mellifluous hand that he should sit with them.

He was enthralled and petrified all at once. Supposing these giants of the underworld rejected him, or beat him up?

But they wouldn't would they, not just like that? They'd listen to what he had to bring to the table at least and, when all was said and done, he'd set out to be just like them – well, for a while at least. He gathered his courage and settled into the seat next to long-nose who didn't so much stiffen as simply remain immovably still.

The taller man had a cultured accent, but Patrick couldn't tell if it was put on or not "You appear to have found Blue Sky, Mr...?"

Patrick was about to say 'Patrick' but realised it was a test. "Moriarty. Er, Moriarty-007," he corrected. The tall man smiled slightly. "Welcome Moriarty, er... 007. You may call me Caesar and the gentleman sitting next to you is Genghis." Genghis' nod was almost imperceptible.

"I take it you would care to join us on our next jaunt, but before we can consider that, perhaps you would care to tell us a little more about yourself and why you joined Blue Sky?" Caesar leant back and folded his arms – not in a judgemental way Patrick thought, but in a 'we haven't made our minds up about you yet' sort of way.

Patrick took a quick look around the pub. It was still heaving but no one was paying them any attention. He'd waited for this moment for years, but he didn't want to appear too eager and took a slug of Blue Sky before answering – and was horrified when some of it fell out of his mouth into his beard. His companions appeared not to notice.

He took a breath and the story came out in something of a rush, "I always wanted to take part in a big job, you know, like a bank robbery or a security truck or somefin', if only someone would ask! I'd do it once and do it big so I was pretty well set up for life, and then never need to do it again. I ain't greedy. That way it would be almost impossible for the cops to catch me 'cause even if I left DNA, there'd be no way to trace me 'cause I haven't got a record and they'd have no reason to suspect me. I know I've got the bottle to go through wiv it and the brains too. I'd even sit on the dosh for a year or two if necessary 'til everyfin' cools off. I can be patient."

There, he thought proudly, he'd said it! He'd told experienced hoods the one thing that'd been on his mind for years. He could be a safe and solid member of the team, turn his hand to anything – except shooting someone. He'd better make that clear he thought. "I don't mind what you want me to do, but I don't want to shoot no one." That was better. That made it clear.

Caesar unclasped his arms and leant forward with a more genuine smile, "Well, Moriarty, you've been very honest with us." Patrick noticed he'd dropped the '007' and took it as a good sign. Even Genghis seemed slightly less solid. Patrick made a fair attempt at holding Caesar's gaze and reached for his own drink, careful to note where his mouth was this time.

"For our part you can rest assured that we have considerable experience in the, er… crime field and would need to consider carefully what role we would need you for. The, ah, project is local and you appear to be a capable young man. It occurs to me that you might be suitable as a distraction runner?" He raised his eyebrows as if waiting to hear what Patrick thought, but after his initial introduction his mind had turned to glue and he couldn't think what the man meant. Fortunately Caesar appeared to recognise this and explained, "Once the police are alerted to our… er, activities, you will move swiftly away from the crime scene as a diversion. They will hopefully follow you and not the real… I mean the rest of the gang who will exit by a different route. Does that sound like something you would be able to do?"

Patrick gave it some thought. He was pretty nifty on his bike. He could weave in and out of traffic with the best of them and knew some really useful shortcuts. They'd have to sort out a route of course, and somewhere he could stash the bike and mingle with the crowd if necessary, but he reckoned he could outpace a few filth over a couple of miles.

"Probably," he answered. "As long as I don't have to carry anyfin' too 'eavy. I mean I'd have to look like I'm carrying loot even if I'm not, wouldn't I?"

Caesar was baffled until he remembered the rucksack with the cycle gear stuffed down by the boy's feet. "Ah! You're thinking a getaway by bicycle. I'd been thinking more in terms of a car, but a bicycle's not a bad idea thinking about it. I can see you're going to be very useful to the team."

Patrick almost exploded with pride. The ideas were coming thick and fast now. "I could stuff my rucksack wiv' bubblewrap. That'd make it bulge out nicely, but would scarcely weigh anyfin', and…"

Genghis decided to interject at this point. Stirring his square bulk towards Patrick he announced solemnly, "We don't do fuck-ups. The Blue Sky Club does it properly – RIGHT?" Patrick looked between Genghis and Caesar in terror and tried to swallow the golf ball in his throat, but the taller man merely smiled and shrugged amiably. "Don't worry about Genghis here. He gets very protective of our little plans, but he does have a point," he went on seriously, "we're not at home to Mr Botch-job, Moriarty. We like to think things through properly and we're very good at it. Now, about remuneration…" Patrick relaxed a bit although Genghis still seemed to be paying close attention even though he'd turned back to his drink.

"We will provide you with a small sum for equipment and so on which you will be expected to obtain yourself. Assuming our current venture is a success, your fee will be twenty five thousand pounds. Does this sound satisfactory to you?" Patrick was disappointed he wasn't being offered more, but had a feeling, 'No I was hoping for a couple of hundred grand' wasn't the answer they were anticipating and, well, twenty five grand was twenty five grand. He could do a lot with that. He nodded reluctantly. If Caesar noticed the lack of eagerness he didn't show it.

"Good. Well, we'll be in touch by email in the next two or three days with the details. In the meantime...?" He glanced at Genghis who sucked his teeth in affirmation. "Please don't let us detain you further."

In some ways the meeting had been a bit of an anti-climax, on the other hand he was in! Patrick left the Dog and Rocket casually, keeping his facial expression neutral. He didn't want to look like an amateur. Fortunately his bike was still chained to the lamp post and still had its wheels. Unfortunately it no longer had its saddle. He sighed and prepared himself for the uncomfortable ride home.

Back in the booth the shorter man turned to the taller one and asked sourly, "You reckon he'll do?"

"Oh, yes! I'm sure he will. If he gets caught there's no way he could lead the Met back to us. It's not as though our descriptions are in the database, is it?" He chuckled gently. "Which reminds me, you'd better take down the website before the raid. And, in the unlikely event he manages to get away, we'll get one of the boys to slip him a couple of grand – and a few broken ribs if he balks at it."

Caesar sat back. He was satisfied with how the evening had gone. The boy was a twit of course, but he'd have the Met chasing their tails for weeks.

He looked across at his cantankerous partner's empty bottle. "Another Blue Sky, Sergeant?"

Springtime

Maithreyi Nandakumar

When G, the long lost cousin, turned up in our lives one May, it was a particularly vibrant spring. We dragged the chairs out of the shed and let the warmth seep straight into the cockles of our hearts. Our raucous laughter was imitated by the birds around us. As the breeze blew in the mellow afternoon, the cherry tree above showered down with pink blossom.

We felt blessed. The relationship between my husband and G was shaped until now by the squabbles of their respective parents. Reinventing this old bond felt thrilling in every way – "After all these years," we said.

"5000 miles away from home, that too," he said.

"Incredible," we agreed, sipping more wine.

The two cousins bonded – G played the guitar and husband the harmonica and we had a feast – food that reminded us of home and other parts of the world that we yearned to visit. We had no family in England and with each passing year felt more distant from our Indian roots. We looked around the small table at each other and found that we couldn't stop smiling.

G lived in Mumbai where he had a successful business. He'd been to boarding school in Somerset and was here for a grand reunion. He could hold forth on any topic under the sun and combine it with bombast and bluster, finishing off with a booming power laugh. We were amused and charmed. He tried to be a sensitive guest and went outside to smoke. However, he insisted we keep him company when he wanted a puff and that was quite often.

"My wife asked me to get rid of my cigarettes," he told us seriously, as if dwelling on the many ills of tobacco. "So, I decided to smoke a pipe," he said with a cheeky grin. After a couple of days, we were relieved that he had friends visit him in our garden, so that we could get on with our work.

"It's amazing, they're all still the same, even after thirty years. We've just resumed where we left off," G was almost effervescent with the thrill of it. Off he went to his re-union – a proud alumnus in a smart suit, silk shirt and maroon school-tie.

He would come into the kitchen to make himself strong coffee and empty his tobacco grounds in the compost caddy. I smelt his strong cologne. Mingled with the pungent pipe smoke, it made my stomach do a backflip.

"You have such fantastic plants – there's nothing more wonderful than an English garden," he would say, disarming me in an instant. I preened but also heard nostalgia in his voice. I tried to imagine how it must've been to spend seven years of secondary school in a strange country away from home.

G made a habit of turning up in May, and the charm began to tarnish a little. In my head, he became a self-inflating mattress which had a pinprick of a hole somewhere in the vast middle. The more you pumped it, the quicker it deflated. Especially as so much of it was hot air, we felt the gust of it surely and strongly. I wished he'd disappear and do his expostulating somewhere else. But my husband who had always looked up to him liked his company when he showed up every year. We never knew why he came so regularly until he let slip that this was some sort of business expense which gave him tax relief.

Last year, I remember dreading the start of May, until he showed up and made a grand announcement. "Take the week off – I've booked us rooms in a grand palace in Istanbul."

As if. "What about your wife – won't she want to come too?" we asked. We'd understood that she was the brains behind the company.

"Nah," he said. "She's much too busy looking after the family firm," he chuckled. His chest visibly expanded with pride as he spoke about their advertising business – their main client, a big tobacco multi-national.

So there we were, on a Turkish Airlines flight to "Byzantium", as he declared, pulling out yet another obscure piece of ancient history, and showing off his Latin. I was beginning to see him as an Indian Boris Johnson. This was not the time to fulminate, I thought piously.

G ate his beef with great relish while we stuck to being firm vegetarians and enjoyed the rigatoni swirling in a delicious aubergine sauce. On landing, Istanbul airport felt like any medium-sized European destination, but with a tangible eastern feel to it.

"It's not that dissimilar to New Delhi," he said with that burst of patriotic pride, as we went out to queue for a taxi. That always caught us by surprise. The orderly nature of things so far was in direct contrast to the chaos of India, but I decided not to contradict him.

Our turn came and the cabbie jumped out, his face lighting up on seeing us. He was eager to talk because we were Indian and then we did feel we were back in Delhi. The night sky was illuminated by the lights of graceful minarets and plump domes. All along the water, the waves shimmered gentle and seductive. I was utterly captivated.

The place that G had chosen was something straight out of Aladdin's tales or as I would later discover, the grand chambers of the Dolmabahce Palace. Sultan's Suites, it was called and G insisted we stay in the best apartment – three inter-linked rooms, opulently designed with a vast gilt-edged, stand-alone mirror in the middle.

There was gory history all over this grand city – the harem intrigues at the Top Kapi Palace and the legendary fratricide of the half-brothers who posed a threat to the throne at the Hagia Sofia. Outside, we got used to hawkers trying to sell us tourist tat, "You're from India? Please, call me Shahrukh," after the Bollywood heartthrob.

G would abandon us at odd times and reappear, but always know where to find us, which seemed spooky in this big city teeming with people.

"Oh, it's probably some app on his tablet," my husband said, dismissing it as an obvious trick.

He insisted we go up the Galata tower – the views he said were stunning, but my husband chose to stay below. The scene outside our penthouse apartment was good enough for him, he said.

Inside the lift, G and I looked at each other and smiled. I'd become fond of him again, as inviting us here was such a generous gesture. His eyes twinkled and he put his arm over my shoulder, hugging me to his side. He winked at me, and I grinned back.

At the top of the winding staircase, I breathed the fresh air and took in the splendour of the Bosphorous and the mosques dotted along the Marmaras and the Black Sea, from high above. I stepped away from the edge – my head reeling a little from vertigo or perhaps the recent contact with G's potent cologne. With my new zoom lens, I snapped away at the different landscapes in front of me and followed the slow line of tourists around, noticing the uneven stone floor. Galata was such a fabulous name – it meant having a party in Tamil. I tried to spot the hubby below but only saw a group of older people dressed in traditional clothes, engaged in a graceful dance. I looked around for G, and saw him having a conversation with someone in a brown leather jacket. He caught my eye and moved away from the man casually, busying himself by removing his glasses and replacing them with his shades and ignoring me. Typical, I thought, intending to mention it to my husband when we went down.

G was nowhere to be seen as I came back to the only doorway. I got to the next level below to what the guide book described as the cleanest toilet in Istanbul, and still seeing no sign of him, took the lift down to the ground floor. My husband was watching the end of the dance. It was a little show being put on for tourists. I felt disappointed to have missed it.

"Where's G?" I asked.

"How would I know? You were with him."

We walked through the commercial area near the tower and found ourselves in a shopping complex – small shops selling watches, cameras and in the corridors, the ubiquitous stalls selling fresh juice. I ordered a pomegranate and watched the man slice the fruit in half and use an old-fashioned press. The small glass of dark ruby liquid confirmed that we were somewhere exotic. We lingered after our refreshment, when my eye caught something a little further away, "Look at that place," I said, quite struck. The store across from us had a large display of rifles, pistols and revolvers. "Have you ever seen anything like it?" Arms and ammunition freely available just like handmade soap or baklava. I began to click the James Bond type pistols and the meaner looking machine guns. Kalashnikovs, AK 47s, I murmured to myself, exhausting my knowledge of such weaponry. I focussed my camera again and my hand slipped for a moment at the sight in my viewfinder. There was G talking to the shop owner, the man in the brown jacket from the tower. G's face was serious and he was ticking off items from a clip-pad. I clicked some more and showed the last picture to my husband. I watched as he registered his cousin's face.

Husband placed his hand at my back and urged me to move. "Enough, we've seen enough – let's go," he said. The metro station was just outside the mall.

We slotted the orange tokens at the turnstile and boarded the train, heaving a sigh of relief at leaving the scene we'd just witnessed. G hadn't seen us and that was good.

We saw him briefly the next morning as we packed up to leave – he was heading east to India and we were going back to England. By unspoken agreement, husband and I didn't talk about him after returning home.

That following Easter, I began to fret about a prospective visit. I asked my husband what he really thought of his cousin, "He's a hustler – we won't be able to understand," he replied, cryptic as ever.

I open the back door to the garden, standing barefoot on the damp grass. Inside, G is on the phone. I can hear husband's polite chuckles and lowered voice telling him that we were not around this year – as we were off on a long holiday to the rainforest in Indonesia. I heard husband say, "Vipers?" and a long interchange about ghastly rituals that used snake poison by indigenous people. Husband's laughing out loud by the end of the chat – the affection mingled with regret in his voice is unmistakeable. And then I hear him ask in a diffident but firm tone, "So, how's business – any more trips to Istanbul?"

I don't want to know and walk out of earshot, to the bottom of the garden. The birds sound a little muted and the mighty cherry tree has been brought down after the storms at the beginning of the year. Bluebells in dense profusion form ripples of purple everywhere, uninvited but welcome guests.

A Trip Like That

Suzanna Stanbury

I'd been about to head out to lunch when the front desk buzzed through to tell me two girls had come into the station and needed to be interviewed.

My dreams of a spicy chicken wrap faded away as I pushed open the door to reception and heard a reedy voice piping.

"That's Lauren Bailey and her cousin Jeanette." Constable Dave Fean nodded at the girl doing all the talking.

"Is Jeanette a Bailey as well?" I asked, as he handed me their incomplete form.

"Yes, Jeanette *is* a Bailey. Our dads are brothers... we always joke that my dad's the clever one as he works out the bus timetables and Jeanette's dad drives them... the buses, that is, not the timetables..."

Lauren Bailey carried on talking as I escorted the girls into an interview room; by contrast, her cousin Jeanette trailed silently after her, head down staring at the scarred grey floor.

"...and I said to Jeanette we've got to take this to the police... but she didn't seem to understand, I tried telling her..." Lauren sat down far too heavily, knocking all the air out of her gizzard.

My stomach decided to fill the silence with an ominous rumble. I watched Jeanette perch nervously on the edge of a seat, as if she thought she may have to take flight at any moment.

"Are you okay, Jeanette? Would you like some water?"

She shook her head at me, hair bouncing away from her face.

"I'll tell you what happened," said Lauren. "I don't think Jeanette's quite sure. Well, I'm not really... Anyway it all started because Jeanette wanted a boyfriend..."

Lauren had immaculate hair, every strand straightened, serumed; perfect lines of blonde streaked in. Jeanette's curly hair looked natural and from what I could see of her face there was little, or no make-up present. She was staring at the veneered table-top as if it was the most interesting thing in the world, listening to her cousin telling me how, she, Jeanette was hopeless on the dating scene, a disaster at attracting potential mates, according to Lauren she wasn't able to catch a man, let alone keep one.

"...and I told Jeanette, that it's when you least expect to get a boyfriend that one turns up."

"You met someone, did you, Jeanette?" I cut in quickly before Lauren could take another breath.

Slowly Jeanette raised her head to look at me and nodded, and then she looked straight back down again.

"What's your boyfriend's name, Jeanette?"

"John Regal," said Lauren. "She was smitten with him, I hardly ever saw her after that... they went on loads of dates..." Lauren gave her small gold earring a flick to straighten it. "And then he asked her to go on holiday... to San Francisco."

"And you went, did you, Jeanette?"

"Oh, yes, she went alright." Lauren rubbed her hands together. "She wasn't going to turn down a trip like that; she's not been further than Tenerife. Tell her, Jeanette, go on."

Jeanette's face came up like a reluctant sun on a winter's morning. "We had a wonderful time," she said, bottom lip quivering as she spoke. "John said we had to experience the place for ourselves and not go on tacky tours. He found us a favourite restaurant overlooking the bay; you could see the lights from the Golden Gate bridge shining down on the water; just like white lightening, John said it was. He had lots of places planned for us to visit..." her voice trailed away, her expression a mask of misery.

I looked back at Lauren; she was biting her lip. "And then John died," she said.

I almost dropped my pen. "What?" I said. "How did he die?"

"Well…" Lauren shimmied forward on her seat. "Jeanette woke up one morning and John'd left a note on her pillow saying he was going out to buy her something."

"A ring…" said Jeanette.

"You don't know that," said Lauren. "He put in the note he was getting you 'something special' *not* an engagement ring. Jeanette was just starting to get worried about where he was when the police rang her and said he'd been run over by a tram."

"It was a cable-car," said Jeanette. "They call them cable-cars, not trams. John said we had to get that right; they're not trams, he said."

"All right – he got killed by a cable-car then," said Lauren.

"Was it an accident?" I asked.

"The police said it was… that's what they told you, isn't it?"

Jeanette nodded. "I couldn't believe it," she said. "I still can't believe it. I keep thinking I see him everywhere I look."

"Jeanette went to pieces, Auntie Elaine… that's her mum… she had to fly over and help sort out the death stuff."

"Formalities," said Jeanette.

"Shouldn't his family have done that?" I asked. "The British Consulate would surely have contacted them."

"John didn't have any family… or any friends," said Lauren. "I thought that was a bit weird when I found out."

80

"He had me," said Jeanette. "John said he loved me more than any girl he'd ever known, and that's how I know he was going to buy me a ring."

I thought for a moment Lauren was looking at me; but she wasn't; her mind was clearly far away; chewing through something like a tough piece of meat.

"So our family had to do everything," she said, her gaze coming back into focus. "And one of those things was to go to his flat and think about clearing it all out…"

Jeanette let out a sob. Her eyes were streaming with tears. I shoved the box of tissues on the table towards her; she grabbed a few to wipe her eyes then balled them up in the palm of her hand.

"And then we found these," said Lauren, "well, I found them really, on a shelf in the living room."

When they came in, Lauren had been carrying a Tesco Bag-For-Life. It had gone under her chair when she fell in it. Now she pulled the bag out, tipped its contents onto the table. Five photo albums slid out in front of us, stopping just shy of the tissue box. Jeanette's spine went rigid when she saw the folders.

A sense of unease gripped me; I shook off the shivers racing down my back.

"This was the first one I looked at," said Lauren, opening it. "There, see: Lucy Westcott."

A photo-booth snap of a brunette in her early twenties was at the top of the page. Underneath was a piece of paper with her name and some very personal details set out in small neat handwriting.

"That's not right, is it?" said Lauren.

I pried the album very gently from her grip. She'd stopped talking and was looking intently at the photo. "It's all crap after that," she said.

The other slots for photos in the album had been filled with various receipts, tickets and flyers from bands and events.

"Look at that," said Lauren, her finger stabbing at the last page. It held a clipping from a newspaper showing a story of an, as yet, unidentified girl found drowned in Lake Windermere; the report stated it was suspected she'd fallen from the path. "Awful," said Lauren. "That's her, I reckon. Lucy Westcott."

Jeanette cried harder. She was picking bits from her ball of tissues; rolling them between her fingers. Lauren got out of her seat; put her palm over her cousin's hands and gave them a squeeze. "It'll be all right now, we're here, aren't we, eh? This nice police lady will make sense of it all."

The next two albums were versions of Kelly Westcott's folder, different girls, similar looking, each with a newspaper report of a girl's untimely death at the back. One girl had been discovered in the French Pyrenees. She'd fallen to her death, it said; and what the vultures had left had to be winched out of a deep pass.

"That's the one you want to look at next," said Lauren, pointing. "The green one."

Jeanette whimpered. I flipped the cover and saw a picture of her, Jeanette, beaming away happily, dark brown eyes crinkled into her smile. There were intimate details written out just like in the other folders. A quick flick through the pages had a few bits of paper marking the passage through her and John's brief dating history but of course there was no more, because John wasn't around to finish it.

"And that's all the albums you found at the flat is it? Lauren?"

Lauren was crouching by Jeanette, her arm around her cousin's shoulder. "What? No. There were quite a few more. But John only had one carrier bag in his kitchen and that's all the folders I could fit in."

Underground

Carolyn Stubbs

Urgent shouts and screams penetrate the eastbound platform of the District Line.

An alarm bell is ringing and someone shouts, "Quick, call an ambulance". A large crowd has gathered at the platform edge. Keith races away from the noise and chaos. Tearing past the bottom of the escalators he heads for the westbound platform. He clutches a woman's expensive looking leather handbag to his chest as he pushes past the other commuters.

Nervously looking over his shoulder he sprints past a woman and child, almost knocking them sideways in his haste, and reaches the westbound platform breathlessly.

"Hey, watch out," she shouts, pulling the child closer to her. But Keith seems oblivious, ignoring them completely. Angela clasps her daughter's hand tight and reads the sign, *'Train now approaching platform five is the 15:15hr train to Wimbledon'.*

As the train pulls up and the doors open, an automated voice warns, *'Mind the gap'* as passengers disembark and alight. Keith scrambles aboard, anxiously checking over his shoulder as if he was checking to see if he was being followed. Angela and her young daughter Penny, who Keith had almost knocked over minutes before, get on behind him and sit down near the door. Angela glowers at Keith but he's clearly distracted and makes no eye contact.

Just as the doors are about to close, a teenager with hooded top and baggy jeans jumps on. Two of his friends don't make it in time as the hydraulic doors clamp together with a hiss. "Wait for us at the next station," shouts one of them, laughing and pulling faces at their friend as the train begins to move off. The teenager inside gives them a 'thumbs-up' then sprawls out on the seat, pulling his iPod from his pocket and pushing in the earplugs.

The train moves from the station immediately and enters the tunnel. The dim lights of the carriage cast blurred shafts of light onto the old blackened tunnel walls as it picks up speed.

Keith looks about thirty-five; he's unshaven, with lank brown hair hanging in limp strands around his face. His ill-fitting jeans are grubby and crumpled, his denim jacket tired and worn. Around his neck hangs a thin silver crucifix dangling on a short chain.

As Keith's laboured breathing begins to come under control, he quickly scans the other occupants in the carriage. It's unusually empty – a middle-aged businessman in a dark suit, bulging briefcase by his feet, reads the free Metro. Next to him are Angela and her daughter Penny, who has since started to look tearful. Opposite Keith is an attractive young woman, somewhere in her twenties wearing a short skirt and cropped jacket. She looks over at him curiously then returns to scrolling through her mobile phone. Furthest away, next to the partition door of the adjoining carriage is another young woman. The magazine she is reading obscures part of her face, and a curtain of long red hair hides her features.

Keith avoids the gaze of the other passengers and clumsily pulls his jacket across the handbag, as if trying to make it look less conspicuous. However, the bag still sticks out quite noticeably and the designer handbag's glossy logo is very evident.

The attractive young woman opposite watches him suspiciously; giving him furtive glances as Keith crosses his legs and uncrosses his legs, while shifting restlessly in his seat.

"I like your bag," she says mockingly, "Prada isn't it? Real expensive."

Keith reddens slightly and looks shifty. "Yeah – well, it's a present for my girlfriend."

"She's lucky you've got such good taste," she smirks, staring at Keith's grubby jeans and his worn jacket. Keith looks the other way, ignoring her remarks as she starts playing with her phone again.

The length of time getting to the next station seems to be lasting much longer than usual. He'd travelled this route many times before, sensing the tunnel's presence but never really taken note of it. He'd never timed how long it took to get to the next station, but instinctively knew it would have been only four or five minutes at the very most. It was three-fifteen when he boarded the train: looking at his watch he was shocked to see it was now three thirty one!

Penny is clearly upset and Keith can see tears running down her cheeks as her mother puts a comforting arm around her. "Try not to think about it, my darling," she says. "You shouldn't have to see something like that, it was just a terrible accident."

"But he pushed her," said Penny, "I saw him."

The businessman looks up from his paper, concern on his face, "Is everything all right?" he asks.

Angela pauses for a moment, swallows hard and looks distressed. She shakes her head to some question the businessman had asked, then points in the direction the train had left from. "... think she must have died... fell or pushed..."

Keith only hears snatches of their conversation as the noise of the train thundering through the tunnel drowns out most of their words. The speed seems to be increasing, along with an accompanying deafening noise as the metal wheels hurtle along the tracks.

"That's terrible – when, just now?" asks the businessman, folding up his newspaper.

"She was only young, about seventeen." Keith thought he heard her saying.

Angela looks pale saying, "... taken by surprise..." The loud rattling sounds of the train's wheels make it difficult to hear every word. "... impossible to survive ... live track," she gasps.

"That's him, Mummy," says Penny looking directly at Keith. She whispers something else to her mother. Angela appears visibly shaken. The three of them give a Keith a hostile stare.

"We *have* to alert the authorities as soon as we reach the next station," the businessman says.

The teenager isn't paying any attention to the people around him, immersed in his own world; his head bobs up and down to the beat of the music in his ears.

The young woman sitting furthest away in the carriage appears pre-occupied with reading her magazine, seemingly unaware of the tense atmosphere that's developing within the carriage.

Keith still looks nervous and reaches into the pocket of his jeans pulling out a small brown medicine bottle. Unscrewing the cap, he tosses a couple of white pills in his mouth and swallows hard. Suddenly the train lurches, rocking from left to right as it picks up even more speed. Just as that happens the medicine bottle slips from Keith's fingers and falls to the floor of the carriage, along with the handbag, spilling out its entire contents. He bends down immediately, reaching out as a lipstick, keys, purse and driving licence slide into a heap onto the floor.

The woman opposite reaches down and picks up the lipstick and driving licence, it shows a photo of a young woman with long red hair named as Lisa Andrews. Before she has a chance to study it further, Keith roughly snatches it out of her hand saying, "Just leave it will you? I can manage."

"I was only trying to help," she says.

Beads of sweat break out over his forehead as he shoves the contents back in the handbag. He leaves the scattered white pills where they are, retrieving only the brown medicine bottle.

Taken aback by Keith's aggressive manner and the obvious lie about the bag being a gift, the woman recoils and sits back in her seat, momentarily lost for words.

Recovering her composure she begins to feel angry and decides to quiz Keith about the bag – his actions are highly suspicious, especially in light of there having been some kind of incident back at the station.

"I thought you said the bag was a surprise for your girlfriend," she says, "but, I see it's got someone else's personal stuff in it."

"Don't have to explain anything to you – Lisa's my girlfriend so mind your own bloody business," he snarls and then moves a few seats away from her.

A sudden jolt distracts attention away from Keith. Unexpectedly the train starts building up even more speed. The current of air coming in from one of the open windows creates powerful gusts, pieces of paper and other debris are tossed about and the carriage lurches in an unfamiliar way. The teenager unplugs his earphones and looks around. He gets up on his feet to look at the underground map displayed on the interior of the carriage. "Hey," he exclaims, looking at the others. "We should have stopped by now – right?"

The businessman checks his watch then tries to peer out at the black tunnel walls as they flash past. "This is very odd," he says. "I can't think why we haven't reached the next station yet. We should have stopped more than ten minutes ago. Mobiles don't work down here either, so we can't ring anyone."

"What do you think's happening?" The young woman asks nervously, biting her bottom lip, but he just shrugs his shoulders at her in puzzlement. The lights flicker on and off as the train hurtles along. The train begins rocking dangerously fast and Penny lets out a scream as the wheels screech and the carriage shakes uncontrollably. The businessman's bulging briefcase is tossed on its side, at the same time the lights start flickering, suddenly go out completely then come back on again, only far less bright than they'd been before.

"What the bloody hell's going on?" the businessman shouts in panic, retrieving his briefcase and trying to peer out of the window but blackness is all he can see.

"I've had enough of this," Keith blurts out getting up from his seat. Reeling against the rocking motion, he stumbles over to the red emergency handle and pulls it down hard. The others look on in dismay but no one speaks. Yet instead of screeching brakes, a sharp reduction in speed that forces an emergency stop, the train continues its relentless journey. The teenager dashes over to where Keith is standing in sheer disbelief. Shoving Keith out of the way he grabs the emergency handle from him, pushes it back to the upright position and pulls it down again hard, but it makes no difference.

The train continues increasing its impossible speed, shaking and rattling as it twists and turns along its horrific journey. The noise becomes almost unbearable. An empty plastic cup rolls rapidly back and forth on the floor, and the lights begin to dim once more. The teenager manages to sit back down, he's trembling, his eyes bright with fear. The girl with the long red hair at the end of the carriage appears strangely unmoved by what's occurring, her face still obscured from view as she bizarrely continues to read.

All of a sudden, a crackling voice over the intercom can be heard above the noise and tumult of the train.

"This is a passenger announcement. Please be advised that this train will NOT be stopping. I repeat this train will NOT be stopping."

Everyone looks at each other in silence before Angela screams and her daughter Penny sobs uncontrollably. The teenager jumps up and begins kicking the connecting doors. "Let us out of here you wankers. *Help, Help.*"

***

Keith closes his eyes and runs shaking hands through his greasy hair, trying to make sense of the inexplicable living nightmare that's come from no-where. Suddenly he's aware that everything's gone quiet. The train is still speeding along but the noise has gone.

The other passengers have stopped shouting, stopped crying out and an eerie silence is now shrouding the carriage. Opening his eyes he stares in disbelief, standing up he looks around him. The other passengers are still there, but they've become virtually indistinguishable. An opaque, yellowish, but impenetrable film has somehow separated them from him. It's as if in they are in another dimension. They still appear agitated, but he can't hear a thing. Is he dreaming? Nausea rises in his throat as he grapples with this bizarre experience. Nervously fingering his silver crucifix, at a loss to know what to do he walks towards them, calling out but they can't hear him. They don't seem to be able to see him either. Strangely he becomes aware that the young woman reading the magazine at the far end of the carriage is missing. She isn't with the others. Some instinct makes him turn round and there she is, sitting just a few seats away.

He can see her clearly, the only other person not shielded by that strange impenetrable barrier.

Resting her magazine on her lap she says, "Hello Keith." Long red hair frames a pale face of a young girl.

"How do you know my name?"

She smiles but doesn't reply immediately, just stares at him with an intense look in her eyes. He's seen her somewhere before he's sure of it, then gasps in disbelief.

It's Lisa Andrews, the owner of the handbag, the one he's still holding, her driving licence photo is now registered on his mind as he stares back at her.

"You know who I am now, don't you, Keith?" she says softly. "You're holding my handbag. You didn't seem to care what happened to me back there, did you? Cared whether I lived or died."

Keith couldn't believe he was having this conversation. Was she a ghost? Had she somehow survived the fall? But her clothes were immaculate and showed no signs of damage.

"I didn't mean for you to fall. It was an accident honestly," he stutters. "There were too many people in the way and you went over the platform edge so quickly."

"If you didn't mean me to fall, why didn't you help me when I did?" Lisa asks.

"I don't know, I panicked, I was scared and I'm a coward. I feel really bad and have done so since it happened. I'm so, so sorry," he replies sadly, genuine remorse showing on his face.

"Look at you, Keith, you're a mess and prepared to let someone die in order to carry out a petty crime. Isn't it about time you took responsibility for your life and those around you? Do you wear that crucifix so that people will think you're good?" Lisa asks in a mocking tone now.

"No of course not, it belonged to my..." Keith stops; the memory still so painful that he found it difficult to expand. He got up. Looking around he wanted to see if anything had changed. But they were still here, still in this eerie and surreal environment that was making him become almost paralyzed with fear.

"It belonged to your girlfriend. Isn't that what you were going to say?" Lisa continues.

"It doesn't matter – I need to know what's going on here." Keith changed the subject. Bewildered, he looked at the distant misty figures of the other passengers, seemingly caught in another world.

"Sit down Keith," Lisa says, "and talk to me."

Unable to do anything else in this surreal dimension of time and space, he sat down again.

"We were on holiday together, last year in Tibet. We were going to get engaged eventually," said Keith, feeling in a kind of daze. "We loved each other so much. We were taking a bus up into the mountains, it was late afternoon and we'd packed up our stuff so we could stay overnight. Jenny wanted to take pictures for her portfolio – she was good at photography." His voice trailed off at the memory of that day.

"It all happened so suddenly but – we were going round this tight bend when our driver shouted out saying he'd lost control. It all happened in seconds. Everyone screamed and tried to leap off the bus. I managed just in time, I'd got hold of Jenny's hand but..." Tears welled up in Keith's eyes.

"My life doesn't have any purpose to it," he said quietly. "Everything's gone downhill ever since and I don't seem to care about anything anymore."

"So you've turned to crime, is that it? You've immersed yourself into a well of self-pity. What would your girlfriend think of you if she knew?" Lisa persisted. "Would she want this kind of life for you?"

"Thank God she doesn't know," said Keith. "But if it's any consolation, I really didn't want to hurt you. But who? What *are* you?"

"Things in life aren't always as they seem," Lisa says. "We all have a purpose here. One action leads to another, setting up a chain of events that has a ripple effect upon all others. Break that chain and it results in a very different outcome."

"Well, I wish I could break out from my situation. I have never nicked anything in my life before – let alone hurt anyone," said Keith remorsefully. He stood up again as he was finding the conversation so strange and unsettling it was hard to cope. Suddenly there was an unexpected twisting lurch, overbalancing him. Keith shut his eyes momentarily, bracing himself for a fall.

But the fall didn't happen and the motion of the speeding train stopped abruptly. It was replaced by the sound of footsteps and people talking. Upon opening his eyes he found himself walking, not running, towards platform five. There were no alarm bells, no cries for help from the eastbound platform. Looking around him, he could see Angela and her young daughter close behind. The overhead gantry showed the illuminated information panel displaying *'Train now arriving on platform five is the 15:15 hr train to Wimbledon'*. Keith looked down at himself in bewilderment, same old clothes, still wearing his crucifix – but no handbag clutched to his chest.

The train roared in and came to a stop. Confused he stepped on, followed by Angela and her daughter Penny. They looked at him briefly but displayed no signs of recognition. The teenager with the hooded top sprang aboard but his two friends didn't quite make it, just as before. The businessman was there, still reading a newspaper and the attractive woman who was sitting opposite Keith before was in the same place, scrolling through her mobile. Keith let his eyes wander to the end of the carriage. Lisa was there – reading. She looked up briefly from her magazine and smiled, her handbag over her shoulder. The carriage doors closed and the train began to move off.

The Gap

A A Abbott

It was ten o'clock on a Friday evening. Jeb had dragged himself away reluctantly from the White Horse, but business was business. He parked his BMW round the corner from Green Park tube station, fishing in his pocket for coins. Fifteen minutes, that should do it. He tutted at the extortionate cost. Still, he was getting a premium for his wares, as he well knew.

Barry, the doorman at the casino, looked him up and down with disapproval. "It's jacket and tie only, mate," he muttered, standing solid and immovable in front of the entrance. Like Jeb, he was tall and broad-chested. In stature, they might have been twins. There couldn't have been more of a contrast, however, between Jeb's dark good looks and Barry's pale, rough-hewn visage.

Jeb bristled. He always wore a leather jacket, jeans and box-fresh trainers; Barry knew that. "I'm just delivering," he said frostily. "Let me inside the door. It's too public to hand it over in the street. And," he grimaced, "you need to find a spot without cameras, obviously."

Barry shook his head. "The customer wants to see you personally."

Was Barry scared of a sting? Jeb considered walking away. Greed overcame him. He had a grand's worth of gear with him, and he'd been offered half as much again for it. "Okay," he said. "I'll meet him in the gents. But I'm not going home to get changed."

"I suppose I can lend you clothes," Barry grumbled. "The management keep a set just in case one of the high rollers turns up in Hawaiian shorts. It's not for the likes of you, but..."

"That would be 'not for the likes of us', Barry," Jeb pointed out. "You're pond life to the high spenders, the same as me."

Barry scowled. "I was about to say, you'll have to take off that jewellery too."

"All right," Jeb acquiesced. He removed the gold pins from his nose and left ear.

The spare suit Barry retrieved from a cubbyhole next to the door wasn't a bad fit. Jeb still detested it, swearing as he changed his clothes in the spartan staff toilets to which Barry directed him. He roughly knotted the cheap, boring grey tie he'd been given.

Barry looked relieved. "I'll take you up to Mr Al-Shakah."

"Is he a rap star?" Jeb asked, tongue in cheek.

Barry ignored him. "You can manage on your own for five minutes, can't you?" he asked the monosyllabic Romanian who shared door security duties with him. The man grunted his assent.

They took a lift to the second floor, where the gaming tables were located: a dozen of them, variously shaped like lozenges or horseshoes. The huge room, red-painted and low-lit, was buzzing with conversation, concentration, sighs as punters lost and cheers as they won. "Impressed?" Barry asked.

"Not bad for a betting shop," Jeb admitted. His eyes flicked between the young, sexy casino staff and the punters clustered at each table, confidently throwing down gaily coloured chips. He felt himself drawn into the excitement, the chance to win a fortune.

Barry nodded to the nearest table. "That's him."

Al-Shakah was playing roulette with hundred pound chips, bright red circles with the denomination written on them. His skin, like Jeb's, was light brown, and he too was probably in his early thirties, but the similarity ended there. He clearly wasn't a Londoner of mixed race. The gambler had a slight frame and an Arabic appearance. His gaze was fixed on the young blonde croupier, who was smiling and congratulating him as she handed him a pile of chips. Jeb's eyes widened. With one bet, Al-Shakah had won two thousand pounds.

Barry coughed discreetly, caught the gambler's eye and nodded to Jeb. Al-Shakah spoke briefly to the croupier before heading to the toilets.

Jeb followed. Entering a cubicle adjacent to the Arab's, he hissed, "Give me the money."

A bundle of notes appeared from the gap below the partition between the two cubicles. Jeb counted them carefully: exactly fifteen hundred pounds. He passed back a couple of sealed clear plastic bags containing white powder. Listening for the other man to leave, he heard nothing apart from a few sniffs and some heavy breathing. Finally, a strongly accented voice said, "Barry says you can get me a girl."

"That could be arranged," Jeb said, adding, "And Viagra." He knew they were alone. On entering the room, he'd scanned it. It was second nature to him. Sensing another sale, he slipped a packet with a couple of blue pills under the partition.

"I want that one. Kat."

"Sorry?"

"I'll show you."

Jeb unlocked his cubicle, hearing a click as the gambler did the same. Nervously, Jeb followed Al-Shakar to the gaming tables. A couple of metres away from the roulette, Al-Shakar jerked a thumb at the blonde croupier. "Her."

Jeb couldn't fault his taste. She was pretty, her face a perfect oval with creamy skin, green eyes and a wide smile. He guessed she would be in her early twenties, perhaps ten years younger than him. It was too risky though. He'd never met her before. He couldn't simply waltz up to her and ask her if she did foreigners. "I'll get you another girl," he said. "A stunner, even better. It'll cost a grand."

He'd chosen a ridiculous figure. His girls usually charged a hundred, tops. They were young, fresh-faced and biddable, though. He thought Al-Shakah would like that.

The Arab didn't bat an eyelid. "In thirty minutes," he said, and turned to play again.

Jeb shuffled back to the gents to make a phone call. He knew at least one young woman had a shift in a massage parlour at the Elephant. It was close enough for a taxi to bring her to Mayfair in twenty minutes. Arrangements made, he took the lift back to Barry.

The doorman held out his hand. "Two hundred, Jeb."

"What? That's double what we agreed."

Barry raised a bushy eyebrow. "He told me he'd want a girl as well."

Jeb couldn't argue. Trixie would be there at any moment, long-haired, short-skirted, made-up like a princess, out of her mind on her own particular brand of addiction. Jeb had learned everybody had an addiction, a gap in their lives they struggled to fill. It was his job to discover it and satisfy it. He sold Trixie what she desired most; she in turn sold herself to the men who craved what she offered. He handed the cash to Barry and went outside for a cigarette. Trixie's taxi arrived as he flicked the last hot ashes away.

"Tell Mr Al, will you?" Jeb asked Barry.

Barry simply shrugged, indicating that Jeb could tell the Arab himself. There was the small matter of payment too, of course. Bolder now, Jeb ascended in the lift once more.

Al-Shakar noticed his arrival at once. He motioned to Jeb to join him at the table. "Here," the Arab pointed to the chips in front of him. "That will cover the price."

Jeb would admit that arithmetic, or any task that involved more than low cunning or brute force, was not his strong point. However, even he could see there were more than ten of the hundred pound counters laid out in front of him. "Thanks," he said.

Once the Arab had left, Jeb could have cashed in the chips, he knew. The blonde croupier turned a dazzling smile on him, however. "Want to play?" she asked. "Black or red?"

In his youth, merely a decade or so before, Jeb had bet heavily on the horses. It was a habit that, while he wouldn't call it an addiction, had led him to take risks with his friends and finances. He'd sought counselling during the resulting spell in prison. Since then, he'd never been near a racetrack or betting shop. Now, he teetered on the brink, torn between common-sense and the lure of the gaming tables.

Hard work had never appealed to Jeb and the temptation of gaining something for nothing was enough to overcome his scruples. "How can I win big?" he asked.

She laughed. "Well, playing black or red, you simply double your money," she said. "But you can bet on just one number, or two, four, five or six, or a line of them. Then you can win more."

Jeb tried to digest her instructions while hiding his surprise at her voice. It was well-modulated, a hint at a monied background far removed from the poverty of his childhood in Canning Town. Why was someone like her working here? He smiled, charm oozing from every pore. "How old are you, Kat?" he asked, reading her name from the badge on her prim uniform. "That's the number I'll choose, if you come out for a drink with me."

Kat's eyes flashed. She grinned. "You don't ask a lady her age," she said, "but you could try twenty three."

He placed a tower of chips on it. She took bets from other punters and spun the wheel. Jeb watched it, a whirling dervish, numbers and colours blurring together. His heart stopped as the wheel slowed, finally settling on twenty five.

"Bad luck," Kat sympathised.

"Not at all," Jeb replied smoothly, "Because you'll let me take you for a drink now, won't you? How about Tuesday?"

He left with her telephone number. Even the penalty notice he found on his car didn't dent his good humour. Despite the gambling loss, he'd made money on the evening. Better still, he'd met Kat. Al-Shakar, and many more like him, would pay well over the odds for a night with a girl like her. All Jeb need do was learn all about her, understand her vices and fulfil them.

Kat watched him go. She knew he was Barry's friend, and she had a shrewd idea, too, of what he bought and sold. The other croupiers occasionally indulged in drugs to help them through long and boring shifts. She chose to spend her hard-earned cash, and easy credit, elsewhere. Jeb's cheek made her laugh, though. She looked forward to a night of cocktails in the West End at his expense.

Her shift was nearly over. Kat returned to the staff locker room to remove the pristine, heavy cardboard bags from designer boutiques she'd patronised that morning. There was indeed a deep, aching need within her, a black hole she filled with the thrill of buying dresses, shoes and handbags. She shivered with delight, recalling the silky, sequinned garments inside those bags. Nothing Jeb could give her would ever come close.

Handbagged

D A Allen

It's not as if that woman really needed it. She looked as if she was doing OK, with her fancy designer suit. That wasn't from H&M, I can tell you. And those bags cost £1,950; you have to order them specially. I know, I saw them in Hello! Magazine in WH Smiths the other day.

And she'd gone off and left it on the seat. Got a message on her Blackberry or whatever, and rushed outside. That's why it's always worth spending five quid on a coffee now and again. The staff don't like it, they look you up and down. I could see the waiter's lip curl, but I kept my nerve. I've got as much right as anyone.

I had the fiver folded up in the palm of my hand – I didn't walk out without paying, did I? Some-one might notice too soon. Just unfolded it, put it under the cup, walked towards the loo, picked the bag off the seat as I went. Kept it low, close to my body. Near the loo they've got an emergency exit. I was out in a second, not running though, just walking fast. Result!

It's an amazing bag – the leather! Soft as butter. Not like the plastic shit that I get. I should have emptied it and dumped it, of course, but I couldn't. As I walked along, I tried it different ways. The strap over my shoulder, the bag under my arm – felt good. Then I lengthened the strap and wore it across my body, the bag in front, or behind. Then I shortened the strap right up and just dangled it in my hand, like those pictures of Posh in America.

I really enjoyed just walking down the street with that bag. It was like being another person – a rich person. I was proud and happy. I walked down the middle of the pavement with my head up. I had this bloody smile on my face, just the feel of that soft leather and the weight of it made me smile. And people smiled back; they did. They catch your eye like you're both sharing some secret. One bloke getting out of a cab even stood back to let me pass. Stood back to let me pass! And smiling at me all the time. As I get nearer home, a bloke on the corner fruit and veg stall, usually as miserable as sin, just handed me an apple as I went by. Grinning he was, never seen that before in my life. 'Lovely day' he says. He nearly bloody sung it, in fact.

I didn't want to come home, to tell you the truth. I knew that would be it. Just walking down the street with that bag I could pretend – I was on my way to a club; I was meeting Kate Moss. Would the paparazzi be there? Or I was going to meet a lovely man – I shuffled through the celebs, deciding which one. Kit Harington, perhaps? Or lovely Robert Pattinson? I wouldn't throw that Ashley Cole out of bed, either. And all the time, I'm walking head up, and people are smiling at me.

As I got nearer home and the streets got crummier, my heart started to sink. I put the bag up under my arm, the strap across, to keep it safe. I knew Angie would be waking up and starting to grizzle. There was no food in the place. But I had to get back. What I don't need is to get reported and for her to be taken into care. I do love her, and I wouldn't have got the flat without her. But I spend so much time alone in it. And everything costs money, there's never enough.

The bag didn't help there – not much in it, not even a credit card. Some pills, an inhaler, a bit of make-up. I was pissed off about that. The lining was beautiful, with lovely zipped pockets – each zip had a little leather tag on it. Who does all that stuff? There must be people sitting all day doing it all. No wonder they cost a fortune, I thought. But then I found a little label right at the bottom, 'Made in Malaysia.' So you can bet the money isn't going to them. Doesn't make sense, does it? I can't get a job, and can't even feed Angie properly. But these people who sell bags for £2,000 a pop give the job to some-one on the other side of the world.

That bag sat on the table while I walked up and down, comforting little Angie, and I just kept looking at it. The place looked so crap next to it. Furnished with me mum's cast offs, bits friends had given me, charity shop stuff. The only thing bought new was a cheap rug from IKEA, and Dan's dog had thrown up on that last week – you could still see the stain in spite of the 1001. My heart sort of lurched downwards. What am I doing? Where am I going?

I don't usually think like that. Usually, it's just day-to-day. What money do I have, what bills are due – that sort of thing. In winter, it's about how long I can stay out so I don't have to feed that bloody meter, spend on heating. I meet up with mates round some-one's flat once a week, have a laugh, but we take the kids with us. Mum sometimes looks after Angie and I go to the pictures; but only in the afternoons now. Since she got that new bloke, I only leave the baby there when he's at work. There's just something about him. I don't say anything, mind, or I'd never see mum again most likely.

It doesn't do to think about the future. When I'm with the girls and we talk about what might happen, really it's a load of crap to tell you the truth. About a boy we saw in the pub with a nice arse or a nice smile. As if getting together with anyone from round here is going to change anything. Either they haven't got a pot to piss in themselves or they'll end up inside sooner or later. Be nice, though, to have a man to share things with, to chat to: lie in bed at night and talk things through, instead of waking up at 3 o'clock in the morning full of worry. But look at what happened to Jessica and Tamsin. Their blokes drank their money, got them pregnant again, and then pissed off. Not much support and sharing there!

Apart from that it's chat about winning the lottery, getting onto Britain's Got Talent, that sort of thing. Hardly a life plan. It's fantasy, that's what it is. Fairy stories. And people I pass on the street, or see gliding along in their bloody great cars, and they're thinking, 'What shall I buy to wear at the weekend?

Where shall I go on holiday?' They can make plans – go to university, get a decent job, meet a millionaire, whatever. They can do it. I'm just stuck, day-to-day. Getting older. Wondering what the hell will happen to Angie.

But I know what will happen to her. She'll be stuck in the same bloody loop. She'll start out all right, working hard at school. Then she'll start to realise there's no decent jobs out there. She'll want to get a bloke and will go shoplifting just to get a lipstick. Probably get off her head and fall pregnant by a good-looking waste of space one Saturday night. And look at her – calm, beautiful. You can see her working things out, trying to make sense of it all – she's bright as a button. She could do as much as anyone else in the world. She won't get a chance to, though, will she? That's not right, it just isn't. It's not her fault. She's done nothing to deserve that.

Still, it's a lovely bag.

Goldie

Liz Ascott

Bug-eyed, tongues hanging out, the cathedral gargoyles stared across the alley at Sabrina Golden. She stood at the open window searching the crowded square below for her son's mop of white-blond hair.

'Goldie's met another girl,' she chuckled. 'I wonder how long this one will stay.'

Rhoda Clutterbuck sat on the couch frowning down at The Times Crossword Puzzle.

'"Following in order, without interruption",' she read aloud.

'I know,' Sabrina said, absently. 'A permanent relationship, that's what he needs.'

'Got it. Consecutively.'

'Anyway, dear, what was I saying?'

'About your funeral clothes,' Rhoda prompted.

'Oh yes. With relatives popping off like nine pins, one has to be quick off the mark.'

'And you'll wear?'

'Cashmere cardigan, trousers, box jacket, cloche hat, shoes, bag. All black. All couture. Being remembered kindly in the Will depends on grooming.'

Rhoda scanned the Down clues.

'"A laughter-maker, almost, but one who changes colour".'

Appraising her auburn tresses in the mirror, Sabrina continued,

'And the elders have a horror of grey hair, you know. Forever young. That's what I have to be.'

The cathedral bell struck twelve. Rhoda folded her newspaper,

'Heavens. Lunch time already.'

'Why the Gannet Restaurant?' Sabrina grumbled.

Rhoda repeated the Rules.

'A restaurant must be chosen for its people-watching facilities as much as its food. Look around you, dear. Good view of the bar, promising clientele. The House red more than hits the spot and the tapas is excellent.'

Mollified, Sabrina settled into the Game.

'Small-time crook? Informer?'

Rhoda nodded.

'He's waiting for the boss. And here he comes.'

A towering tow-haired man had appeared, and was ambling towards the informant.

Sabrina bit into her spicy aubergine slice.

'Those who inhabit dark corners. What d'you think? A reptile?'

Rhoda nodded.

'The reptile and the ferret.'

As if to read the messenger's lips, the two women craned forward. The reptile blinked his hooded lids and gazed over the heads of the crowd. Then, bending low, he whispered his response. A spasm ran through the ferret's wiry frame. Without a backward glance he ducked into the crowd and vanished.

'Well,' Rhoda said. 'More wine, dear?'

'Wait. Someone else has joined the fray.'

A tall dark young woman carrying a rucksack now stood

beside the reptile at the bar.

Sabrina's hands flew to her cheeks.

'Look,' she gasped.

Astonished, they watched the reptile's back straighten, his chest expand, his dingy dishevelled hair rear up in a golden crest – and a million pinpoints of greenish light play round him.

Rhoda's eyes narrowed.

'That's Goldie,' she said, softly.

'No, dear. It can't be.'

'Oh yes it is.'

In one unbroken movement, Goldie hailed the barman, bought the girl a drink, picked up her rucksack and gently propelled her from the bar.

'Seamless,' Rhoda observed, dryly.

Shaking her head and dabbing at her eyes with a Gannet napkin, Sabrina whimpered,

'Oh Goldie, who are you?'

'He's a forty year old man living at home on an allowance from his mother,' Rhoda snorted. 'That's who he is.'

After lunch the friends strolled home through the Botanical Gardens. Goldie had some sort of magnetic force field at his disposal, Sabrina decided. That would account for all those young women who passed through the house.

'He was a reptile when he walked into the bar,' Rhoda

reminded her.

Sabrina shrugged.

'The boy's clearly all things to all people. It's a gift, really.'

'A chameleon,' Rhoda said, suddenly. '"A laughter-maker, almost, – but one who changes colour".' That's the answer to the Down clue.'

The two women paused to watch a flotilla of hot air balloons drift over the city, their baskets full of waving people. Sabrina felt her spirits lift. The sight of the gaily decorated balloons put her concerns in perspective, somehow. Her only son was a handsome, charismatic scallywag. So what!

On their return to the house, the two women discovered Goldie lying in front of the open window on the second floor.

Rhoda scanned the room, wonderingly.

'Good heavens, the boy's alone. That's a first.'

Sabrina lifted a finger to her lips.

'Hush, he's sleeping.'

The arched eyebrows, the unblinking blue eyes, the mouth formed in a perfect O of surprise – all suggested otherwise to Rhoda.

'No dear, not asleep. Dead,' she said, briskly.

A puzzled expression settled on Sabrina's face. Kneeling beside Goldie, she sandwiched his cooling hand between hers.

'I really don't know what to say, darling. I'm as perplexed by this turn of events as you appear to be. As you know, my social life has always been rather hectic. Never a moment to gain my breath. As for discussing the death of your late father, the Field Marshal...'

Rhoda groaned.

'You don't think, dear...'

'That Goldie might have been involved in the Field Marshal's death?' Sabrina said, a touch sharply. 'Out of the question. Before flinging himself over the edge of the Grand Canyon, the Field Marshal got Goldie to write a farewell note. Imagine that. A seven-year-old boy. I've still got that note somewhere.'

Placing Goldie's hand over the vicinity of his heart, Sabrina rose and stood by the window.

'Those damn gargoyles are staring in again.'

Rhoda pushed a tumbler of whisky at her.

'You're in shock, dear. Get this down you.'

After several attempts at resuscitation, Goldie was borne away by the ambulance men. From the depths of her four-poster bed Sabrina dictated her wishes regarding the funeral.

'My Goldie's life shall be celebrated by all who crossed his path,' she declared. 'We shall gather at Charlton Heath. The worms, not the family vaults, shall have him. And we shall return to the house for the Wake.'

'The Botanical Society will donate a sapling for the tree-planting ceremony. After all I've done for them, they'd bloody well better. Your idea of popping Goldie into cold storage was inspired. He'll be daisy-fresh on the day.'

'Before the funeral can take place, an autopsy will have to be performed,' Rhoda said, gently. 'Let's compose the Obituary, shall we?'

Persistent rain and mist hindered the journey to Charlton Heath. Small groups of hump-backed walkers stuck out their thumbs as Sabrina's taxi passed.

'Waterproof capes over rucksacks,' Rhoda explained. 'Makes 'em look like dromedaries, doesn't it?'

A fleet of limousines raced past. Fish and chips and greasy newspapers were pushed through lowered windows to whirl in the wind and slap against the taxi windscreen.

Charlton Heath Barn smelled of must and tallow. Sabrina in expensive black and Rhoda in moth-eaten velvet, sat close to the bio-degradable whicker coffin at the front.

Faces from the bars and restaurants in town, buskers from the square, girls who had stayed a night and moved on, the ferret and his suited companions – all sat in the rows behind.

After paying her last respects to her son, Sabrina returned to her seat.

120

Rhoda pointed at a trickle of water coursing down the worn striations of the flagstones towards the great oak door.

'Goldie's defrosting, dear.'

Sabrina's shoulders shook; she began to sob.

Rhoda turned to the mourners.

'Right! I need six pallbearers to lift the basket. Now.'

The suited men poured into the aisle, to jostle and buzz round the corpse.

'Meat flies,' Sabrina said, disgustedly.

Rhoda cupped her hands round her mouth.

'I said, lift the bloody basket.'

This second request proved effective. From among their ranks six suited men were selected to shoulder the deceased back down the aisle to the rain-lashed heath.

Severed roots hung from the sliced earth. Worms wriggled and fell on the basket. The girls linked arms and sang that summer's Eurovision song contest entry.

'D'you suppose Goldie was a pop star?' Sabrina asked, hopefully.

When the last shovel-full of earth had been replaced, a Charlton Heath employee stepped forward, holding a sapling.

Rhoda raised an eyebrow.

Sabrina gave a watery smile.

'A monkey puzzle tree. Guaranteed to dwarf everything for

miles around.'

The mourners returned to Sabrina's house for the Wake. The champagne fizzed. The barman from the Gannet proposed incomprehensible toasts. The mourners drank. After towelling their hair, the girls unfolded maps and drew circles round foreign cities. The suited men removed their jackets, rolled up their sleeves and arm-wrestled, grunting and scuffing their feet under the table. But no funny stories were told, no dark secrets revealed.

Rhoda spotted the ferret crouched behind the bar placing bottles of wine in a canvas bag. Arms folded, she loomed over him.

'In some sort of business with Goldie, were you?'

'You could say that, Madam,' the ferret smirked. 'You could say that.'

The cathedral bell tolled the hour. Unrolling their sleeping bags, the girls bade each other goodnight, the suited men departed. Rhoda retired to bed with that day's copy of The Times.

The rain had passed. A full moon presided over harsh light and deep shadows. From the open window, Sabrina could almost taste the perfumed night air.

After the Field Marshal's death she had taken refuge in the house overlooking the square. Goldie had whisked about the shadowy rooms, demanding to be fed at the oddest hours.

Rhoda, who had become a dear trusted friend, had applied for the job of companion/nanny. Goldie had not appreciated her "Sergeant Major" ways. She had not appreciated his practical jokes.

A little boy flicking rows of tin soldiers out of the window floated across her vision. A beautiful young man turned and smiled at her from the empty square.

A slight movement on the cathedral wall caught her eye. But when she looked, the gargoyles were stone cold still. Those sly devils. Always playing games.

'Enough,' she cried.

The Field Marshal's rifle was heavy. She had to rest it on cushions.

The first three bullets wiped the smiles off the gargoyles' faces. The forth bullet brought the Italian ice cream sign across the square crashing down with a clatter on the potted geraniums below.

'Not bad,' she said, standing back to admire the results of her handiwork. 'Not bad at all. Might take this up.'

Gloss

Judy Darley

We spend a couple of hours in Superdrug, playing with nail polish testers until every fingernail is a different glittery colour. Tammy's mouth is a deep plummy purple – so juicy I want to take a lick. She scrubs the gloss off with a tissue, grabs the next, a cerise too pink for her skin tone.

"What d'ya think?" she asks, pursing her lips like she's kissing the air.

Her eyes laugh at me as I stammer out: "So cool!"

Gaze fixed on mine, she snaps the cap on the gloss, stuffs it in her pocket, fast. "Now you."

I can't breathe, but she's watching me. Daring me. Quickly I grab the plummy purple, stick it down my top, into my bra. See admiration and surprise widen her pupils.

We run out of the shop, giggles spilling.

Back home, I slide the lip-gloss from my bra, feel it breast-warm in my hand. I tip it over, read the name: *Bruised Kiss.* I spread it over my lips, pout at myself in the mirror, meet my own thickly mascara-lashed stare. Taste something more bitter than sweet.

The Purple Sensation

Richard M S Kemp

The smell that travelled through the grey offices of Merke Associates was almost as depressing as the company's choice of paint; a brooding, dull absence of colour covered every wall, each one meeting a dusty white skirting board at the bottom. A scent of long-empty fast food containers, crisp packets and muted sweat rose in waves from the company's IT helpdesk, sweeping across the four corners of the open-plan office, picking up nuances of cheap perfume and floor cleaner before arriving at the nostrils of Polly Jacobson.

Polly had worked for three years as an assistant supervisor for Merke Associates. The pay was enough to get by, though she hated the work; sat in front of a computer screen for eight hours, her main job seemed to be forwarding passive-aggressive emails back and forth between middle managers and her colleagues. At least it was far enough away that she could cycle to work. Polly never considered cycling a passion of hers, though that was until she met The Purple Sensation. A sparkly violet 21-speeder with front and rear suspension, mudguards and an extra-loud bell, the Sensation had it all – it even came with a basket on the front and a rubber flower strapped to its handlebars. It wasn't perfect by any stretch, the back brake would never tighten correctly while the middle gear skipped without fail but it was Polly's.

Slumped at her desk connecting one disgruntled employee with another, Polly would often find herself daydreaming of past rides on the Sensation: treks across the Peak District, pootles along coastal pathways and the always-rewarding cycle to a countryside pub for a boozy lunch. Then there was the week-long holiday to Southern Spain with Claire.

Before Claire, Polly had been eating lunch alone, either at her desk or in the company's white-walled cafeteria, however, she rarely did the latter since she would risk running into Shaun Mowerly, a middle manager from Operations. Shaun was a short, pale man, thinly-built with wiry red hair. He seemed convinced of Polly's and his friendship, to the point that he insisted on giving her a new nickname every time he saw her. "Pols!" "Pollster!" "Pol to Pol!" "Pollen Count!"

"Hi, Shaun," she would manage to say.

"How's tricks, then?"

"Oh, you know," Polly would reply, feigning to pick up a novel from her handbag. She always kept a book handy, especially for those quiet lunchtimes or for fending off unwanted visitors. "Nothing much. Just reading."

"What's that?"

"Love In The Time Of Cholera."

"Garcia Marquez? Oh, Polly," Shaun would say before sidling up next to her and pulling out a lunch from his bag. "He's alright, I suppose, though his prose is so flowery."

Polly would normally give an opinionless grunt at this point.

"If you are going to read any Garcia Marquez, at least go for One Hundred Years Of Solitude. That's the classic that everyone should read."

An "mmm-hmmm" would escape Polly around this point followed by a passionless, "Thanks, Shaun. I'll consider that for next time."

"I'll bring it in! Will you be here tomorrow?"

"Probably," which invariably meant "no."

Tired of hiding behind her computer screen at lunchtime, Polly took a chance on Rusty's, a pokey little cafe off the beaten track side of town. There was almost always something questionable wafting through the cafe's greasy front windows and the tables were rarely clean, but there was nothing else close enough to the office, unless someone was willing to drive out to McDonald's. Most people in Rusty's had either come straight from the Merke office or were just leaving to go back. Polly was queuing to pay for a dry cheese sandwich on white bread when she met Claire, a tall blonde woman with wide-rimmed glasses and a pointy nose. She wore a white blouse that was two sizes too big for her and a long, drab, brown skirt that flowed down to her ankles. Claire had just started working at Merke in Accounts and recognised Polly from the other end of the office. Claire introduced herself to Polly and asked how she was finding Merke Associates.

"Could take it or leave it, I suppose. How about you?"

"I'll take it for now," said Claire, smiling.

Polly and Claire were soon getting together at Rusty's on a regular basis to discuss everything from ridiculous requests and self-important managers to incompetent peers and the leery-eyed advances of Shaun Mowerly. They limited their lunch dates to every Thursday since neither could afford nor stomach more than one trip to Rusty's per week.

Though Claire provided some genuine happiness for Polly, it wasn't enough to counteract the guttural sickness that she felt every morning as she walked through the glass double doors and into the starch-filled melodrama of Merke.

"I'm quitting," she told Claire one Thursday over a lukewarm carrot soup.

"Mmm-hmm," Claire replied, sipping on her coffee. "When do you plan on doing this?"

"I mean really, Claire. This is it. I'm sick of their crap."

"Me too. So when are you quitting?"

"I haven't decided yet, but I'm ready. I could go any day now."

"Well at least give me some warning so that I have time to find you a leaving gift."

Polly laughed at this so much that she almost enjoyed the taste of the burnt coriander.

"Seriously though, Pol," said Claire, looking directly into her friend's eyes. "What will you do when you leave? Do you have anything lined up?"

Polly fell back in her chair, holding onto the arms and staring at the ceiling. "Oh, I'll be alright," she said. "I've got some money saved, plus this might be my chance to finally take a holiday."

"That might actually be good for you."

"Yeah, just some time for me. Chill for a while, you know? Really think things through."

Claire downed the rest of her coffee and went to grab her bag. "Sorry, Pol. I've got to head off early. My manager needs some breakdowns by the end of today and there'll be no time otherwise."

Polly gave a wide smile, perhaps a little too wide. "No problem," she managed. "It's good to see you, Claire."

"Same time next week, yeah?" Claire asked, fumbling with her jacket.

"Yeah."

Polly returned to work to complete another four hours of email tennis between her co-workers. She headed out to the bike shed at the end of the day to find the door wide open and The Purple Sensation gone. Polly stood in silence, letting the cool air hang over her and taking in the scene: whoever had stolen her bike had been quick – they were strong, too. Polly's bike had two locks and there was a giant one on the shed itself. Someone had been thinking about this for a while.

No one knew how to ride the Sensation except Polly. Not properly anyway. What would they do when they noticed the back brake was dodgy? What about the middle gear? Would they be patient? Or would they take it out on the bike, kicking it and hammering down on the pedals? Polly began to feel a sickness build inside her, a kind more potent even than the one she felt every morning as she walked into the Merke building. Polly lowered her head into her shoulders and burned with anger. She heard another person behind her; it was Shaun Mowerly. He was wearing a bright orange cycling jersey and a hi-vis vest on top.

"Hi, Pol – oh no, your bike wasn't stolen, was it?"

"Yep," she replied, keeping her gaze on the space where The Purple Sensation used to be.

"I'm sorry. Was it worth much?"

Polly sighed deeply. "No, not much." What did it matter how much money it was worth? "Still, it was mine."

"Yeah, sorry. What kind of lock did you have?"

She winced at this. It wasn't the best lock in the world, far from it, though she had hoped the bike shed door's lock would be enough of a deterrent.

"Just a couple of those cable locks," she replied.

"Yeah, that's why I've got one of these now." Shaun brandished a heavy-duty d-lock and gave it a tap. "Can't be too careful, even if the shed door does have a lock." He thought for a moment. "Was the shed door lock cut, too?"

"Yep."

"Ah. That's too bad. I'm sorry. Oh," he said, pointing to a scratch on his lock, "it looks like they've had a go at mine, too. Next time, I would definitely recommend a d-lock."

"Thanks, Shaun."

"See you tomorrow. Hey – and let me know if you want any help finding another bike. I might know someone who's looking to sell."

"Thanks."

Polly took the number 41 bus home that night; it was a 35-minute journey that would have normally taken her 20 minutes on The Purple Sensation. It wasn't free anymore, either, instead costing £2.50 to go just seven stops. Polly stood there, wobbling over each bump and seething at the busload of losers that surrounded her, the losers who just this morning she was overtaking with a grin on her face. She would have chosen the fumes of the road over the smells inside that bus any day; the sweaty odours rising from her fellow blank-faced travellers made her want to vomit and the thought of having to pay for the privilege every day nearly sent her wild.

The next day, Polly was seething still. She sat at her desk, emailing names back and forth in silence, though bashing her keyboard in an extra-loud fashion. She emailed Claire.

Hi Claire,

I know it's not Thursday, but my bike was nicked last night. Fancy a lunch date today?

Thanks,

Polly x

Within minutes, she had received a reply.

Hi Polly,

Sounds great! Not the bike nicking bit of course. I'm so sorry. Let's meet at Rusty's today.

Best,

Claire x

"I'm quitting," Polly told Claire.

"I know." Claire put her hand on Polly's. "When are you going to tell them?"

"That bastard!" Polly exclaimed, pulling her hand away from Claire's and almost hitting a diner behind her.

Claire sat in silence.

"How dare he... they... whoever!"

"I know."

"Who the hell steals someone's bike? What is wrong with these people? Ugh, I hate this place so much. I have to get out."

Claire took a sip of her coffee.

"Don't they understand what they're taking away?" continued Polly. "It's not just a bloody bike! That bike was part of me."

"Have you filed a police report?"

Polly scratched the left side of her face and sighed. "Yeah, almost. I mean, what's the point? Who's going to go after someone's mountain bike?"

"Well, if you don't file a report, there's no chance they will ever find it."

Polly turned away from Claire at this. "What would they even want with her? She's an old lady for Christ's sake. I feel so dirty now. Who the hell steals someone's bike?" Polly began to well up with tears. "They don't even know how to ride her."

Claire reached for Polly's hand again. "You know, Pol. It was only a bike."

Polly looked at Claire's hand as if it were diseased. "It was more than that."

"I'm sorry," Claire began. "I just meant—"

Polly pulled away from Claire, grabbed her bag and stormed out the door of the cafe.

Polly caught the number 41 bus after work, went straight to the nearest supermarket and then home. She then began the one thing she had wanted to do all day: get horrendously drunk. She connected her mp3 player to her hi-fi and blared out the best of Dionne Warwick for the rest of the night, chiming in with the occasional harmony to "Walk On By" or "Why Do You Have To Be A Heartbreaker?"

Polly awoke the next morning in a thick fug of vodka, rum and coke. She had fallen asleep on the living room sofa after smoking a 20-pack of cheap cigarettes and emptying every booze bottle she had bought. She'd made pizza at some point too, the frozen kind and dropped most of it on the carpet.

Polly rolled over onto her back and then sat up to feel an almighty pounding in her head. She quivered across the sticky carpet to the kitchen and downed two pints of water before throwing them back up into the sink. Polly held tight to the countertop, feeling her knees tremble; this was the kind of hangover that got every part of your body. She walked back through the thick air of yesterday's booze and into the bathroom. The light sprang on and she caught her face in the mirror. Tired and beaten, Polly looked as if all the life had been drained from her. The bright bathroom light brought attention to her pale, white skin and dry, red eyes. She would have cried right there and then had it not been for the chime of a text message.

Hi Polly. I hope you start feeling better soon. I think we should hold off on any more lunch dates for now. Claire x

Polly stood in the bathroom, bathing in the stark light. She scrunched her face, confused, then scrolled up a little to see that she had sent three other texts before the morning's message to her.

21:45

Hi Claire. Thanks for all your support today. I'll remember this for when you lose something that you love. Polly.

22:56

Howdy Claire. Thanks again. You're a real friend. Polly.

02:34

Hi Claire. I'm sorry for the last two messages I sent. They were not nearly clear enough. I'd like you to leave me alone. Take my number out of your contact list and stop pretending to be my friend. It's pathetic. Polly.

Polly shivered at this third text message. She laid her phone on the edge of the bath tub and walked back through to the kitchen. She tried another glass of water and managed to keep this one down. The smells of pizza and cigarettes began to catch up with her and so she went back into the living room to clean up. She knelt to pick up a slice of cold, hard pizza that had fallen face down under the coffee table and saw a photo of her and Claire out on their bikes in southern Spain. An enormous blue sky towered over majestic sandy mountains and perfectly-straight olive groves. There were some orangeries dotted in the distance and a lonely wooden shack. Polly and Claire stood in the foreground, holding onto their bikes with one hand and hugging each other with their other. They were both smiling, beaming with pride. Polly felt the Andalusian breeze rush past her face as she whipped along the hilly roads. The sun, pulsating a white and yellow heat, made every hill-climb a colossal task. This one had been more of a mountain than a hill.

Polly reached the top and set her bike against a flimsy old wooden fence that bowed with the weight. Polly took a slug from her water bottle and, regaining her breath, went to join Claire on a bench.

"This is so beautiful," she said, overlooking the scene.

Claire gave out a sigh. "Yeah, it really is."

"What is that over there?" Polly asked, pointing to the wooden shack. "An outhouse?"

"Who knows? If we wait long enough, we might find out."

"Could be where the farmer stores all his dead bodies!"

"Or where a young buck takes the farmer's daughter!"

"Ooh, scandal!"

Polly looked down and kicked a stone away from them, sending it rolling down the hill.

"So when are you leaving Merke?" asked Claire.

"I don't..." said Polly, moving to kick another stone. "The job's still crap but, well, you know..."

Polly felt a hand on hers. She turned to meet Claire's gaze.

"Hey," said Claire. "I'm really glad you came."

Polly grinned, her eyes widening. "Me too."

Angel on a Road to Nowhere

Nigel Lapworth

I looked out across the fields behind me to where the thin smudge of dawn was beginning to melt into the canopy of the distant tree line. It was cold enough for mist, but there wasn't any today, just a clear view of the world emerging, forcing back the darkness to reveal autumn colours.

I shivered as I finished fuelling up and returned the gas nozzle to the pump. The meter read ninety six dollars which I figured might get me as far as Memphis, or even Little Rock. Maybe. I could only see one security camera pointing towards the cashier's window at the rundown pay booth, but I didn't intend to hold the place up or drive off without paying. You won't get far on these long straight roads before the local Sheriff is in your face. Still, I was glad of my neckerchief and skid-lid. With any luck the kid in the booth would be pretty much the last person I'd have to talk to until I got to where I was going. If he was asked he'd probably recall a tall biker guy. Six three. No distinguishing features. No colours on the back of his jacket. East coast accent. The bike? No fancy customisation, just a regular Harley tourer. Filled two eight-gallon canisters as well as the tank. Had 'em strapped on under canvas panniers, but not so unusual if he was going a pace. Paid in cash. Headed west.

The last trace of gasoline fumes faded away in the crisp air as I made my way to the booth.

I picked up speed until I was just under the legal limit and hit cruise. The bike was loaded up but you wouldn't know it from the engine note. Everything I owned was strapped to the seat behind me, but in truth it didn't amount to much. I'd left everything else back at the Mission three days ago. They could keep it. I was going to have to try to forget the past although I doubted I ever would.

The sun was just beginning to tip the trees now, throwing my shadow forward onto the road, but a full moon to the south followed me stubbornly through the morning like the tip of God's accusing finger.

I didn't want to think, not about anything, but when you're in the saddle for hours you can't help it. It's like insomnia or something. The more you try to get to sleep the less chance there is of making zeds. With riding, the more you empty your mind the more it fills with stuff you'd put behind a locked door. But I couldn't stop yet. I needed to make distance.

The last words the Outrider guy had spoken rattled around my head like a mantra. The moment before everything stopped for him he'd said those words. I'd heard them clear as day even though the sirens had been getting real loud, like we was just passing the time and wasn't bleeding all over the lane behind Hansel's place, or all over me.

"What are you worth, Ariel?" he'd asked. "What are you worth?"

Said it like he really wanted to know. All concerned like Father Hancock used to be before he hung himself, you know? I figured those words would stay with me.

***

The Meet hadn't meant to be some big deal. Just the boys hanging and drinking a few to welcome the new blood to the Chapter. The ball game was loud on the screens up by the pool tables and Jesse kept bringing the beers to our booth further down the bar. As she mopped the table she kept telling us to hush up or Hansel would kick us out. Luke, one of the new bloods, kept trying to slap her ass, but she was too quick for him. They were used to us and knew we didn't look for trouble there or nothing. Pay for any damage too, not that there ever was much. We didn't fight amongst ourselves often and kept the other gangs away too. Well usually.

Jake Mackie had come in, looked around, and slithered our way. "The Outriders want to parley. It's important." He'd said it to the table at large like something out of a cheap western. We were a few beers to the good by then and no one could tell who he was trying to talk to with his eyes always looking all over. Then again, no one in the Pistols had ever given much for Jake Mackie, so no one was really listening anyway. He'd asked to ride with us once, but we told him no, same as all the other crews. He just kept hanging around anyway like he had nowhere else to be. Got to give him credit though, he stayed where he was and repeated his message, this time focussing best he could on Tank.

Now, maybe if he'd talked to me I might have taken it in, but Tank was in no mood to listen that night. He'd started drinking midday and was well on the way to rowdy.

"What's that Slack Mackie? You wanna' shoot the breeze with the Pistols?"

Mackie just stood there with his eyes rolling and remembered not to shuffle his feet just like his momma told him. Tank got up and leant across the table. He's a big man and even leaning forward he was looking down at Mackie, "We don' wanna' hear what you gotta' say Mackie."

His fist came out from under him so fast his other arm had to bend to support his weight, but he still caught Mackie a blow to the temple that sent him tumbling out of the booth and across the floor.

"Smackie!" roared Tank and collapsed back into his seat. We fell about. Funny as fuck. Mackie managed to get himself upright and staggered off towards the door holding a hand up to his face muttering, "Shee'it! Shee'it!" to himself.

But that wasn't the end of it though, because the Outriders took offence. We hadn't noticed, but they'd queued their hogs up outside just waiting for an invite. They'd sent Mackie into Hansel's 'cos he was kinda neutral, but from where they were looking, all we'd done was send him back out with a good slap. Normally one of the boys would stay sober enough to keep point, but that night everyone was in a good mood and trying to have a little fun.

We knew the Outriders had been recruiting recently. Some of the boys they were taking on weren't local brothers, so they had the numbers on us these days.

A few minutes later Crop and two of his Lieutenants came in through the door and looked our way. I thought they were going to come over and start a parley like Mackie had said, but they must have had other ideas that night. Seems they thought they had the better hand and, after eyeballing our booth for a minute Crop signalled the rest of his crew in. They were all wearing denim cut-offs with their colours across the shoulders. Red lettering on a white background, like a uniform you know? Ours look almost the same.

Now there must have been near thirty of them set against ten of us in the booth. They didn't look heavily tooled up and some of them didn't look too business-like, but anyone could see those odds were slim. I guess we could just have walked out, but Hansel's was our place. Slap in the middle of our turf. I couldn't figure it out. Crop had brought all his boys in wearing their colours. Might just as well have declared war and everybody knew it. Jesse looked nervous behind the bar and disappeared out back. We all stood up, waiting to see if Crop would talk or fight. Even then I thought there might be a chance to resolve something, after all, they must have come here for a reason and they'd sent Mackie in first before barging in.

Then we all heard the roar of engines as six more bikes pulled up outside. They were ours. Two of the bikes were two-up although we didn't know it at the time. Eight more Pistols. There was a moment where everyone in the bar hushed up and waited. It was as though time paused before taking its next breath. No one spoke. No one moved.

There was some talk going on outside, but none of us could hear what was being said and then we heard the crash of bikes being kicked over and the hiss of tyres being slashed and then all holy hell broke loose.

***

I pulled off-road to some shelter under a stand of oaks well back from the highway and lit my primus stove to make coffee.

Most would have considered that little primus a luxury, but small comforts can mean a lot on the road and hot coffee always hits the spot for me. Clouds had been building in the west and I'd known I was going to run into them sooner or later, but the downpour had been heavier than I'd expected, so I decided to sit it out for a while. The susurration in the branches above me drowned out most of my thoughts. The state line was more than thirty miles behind me but I still didn't feel confident enough to hitch up my tarp and start drying out clothes and such. That would have to wait. As it was, the trees did a pretty good job of keeping the rain off.

I'd filled the gas tank from one of the cans somewhere around Roanoke, about an hour before making State, and spread the remaining fuel between the two cans to even out the weight. The bike's odometer showed I'd covered around four hundred miles, so I had fuel for about another six hundred. I'd brought food and water just so I didn't need to go getting my face on some Wall Mart spy camera, and the break gave me a chance to take stock and stretch my legs.

I found myself thinking about Father Hancock's sister Rachael. He hadn't been old for an ordained man, and she must have been ten years younger still. Maybe no more than twenty. I'd always had an eye for her even though I would never have dared ask her out. To me the sun had always shone that bit brighter when she'd turned up at the mission to help her brother with the talking and the soup, and I guessed she might even have had an eye for me too. There was a time a smile and the hint of a promise passed between us, at least I thought so. I scarcely talked with her though. I knew she was way better than the likes of me and although Father Hancock had been a good man and only ever wanted to help the crews sort out their shit if he could, it made sense he wouldn't have wanted an Angel as part of his family.

What had happened to her was *bad* bad, and by the hand of a brother too. The Police never found anyone for it that's for sure. No one ever said it, but all the crews had had respect for Father Hancock. Everyone figured one of the gangs was covering, so no one trusted no one. Turned out Father Hancock had no other family than that sister. He must have loved her very much to take his own life that way.

I stood under the canopy and watched little waterfalls tumble off the end of each branch, making puddles that trickled away in brown rivers towards the field behind me. It reminded me somehow of the pure, ice-cold mountain lakes feeding the streams with snow melt. I'd been up in the mountains only two days before, getting rid of the knife. I don't know why it took me so long to find a good place to hide it. I'd ridden for hours.

**

146

Crop barked an order and half his crew flew back out through the door to take on the Pistols out front and rescue their mounts. He led the rest our way, kicking over bar stools to make his point. Most of the other customers were up the other end of the place playing pool or watching the big screens. They'd kept out of our way all evening, but now they stopped to watch. There was no sign of Hansel or Jesse.

Those good old boys didn't have to wait long. Tank charged the advancing Outriders with his arms stretched wide, deliberately aiming for a few of the weaker looking dudes. Looked like he was trying to take out a bunch of them in one go to even up the numbers some. It worked too. He swung his arms in at the last moment bringing two heads together in a crack you would have heard in the next town. His momentum took him into a third who had his back to the bar and had no way to avoid a head butt from the maddened giant. The guy's nose exploded and he crumpled next to the other two, streaming blood onto beige carpet tiles.

The rest of us found someone to fight, like country cousins at a shotgun wedding, those at the back hurling insults and waiting their turn to join in, but the blows raining in hurt real enough. There was damage being done outside too. Among the shouting some of the boys were swinging chains judging by the occasional clang of metal on metal, or the dull thud of another type of contact followed by howls of pain. It sounded as though it was getting serious.

Whatever was happening out there, the fight wasn't going so well for us inside. One of the Outrider Lieutenants had managed to get behind Tank and jerk his leather jacket down his back so he couldn't use his arms. Another brother gave him the good news with alternate fists to his stomach and face. Two more of our boys were curled up on the floor trying to save their teeth from flying boots whilst I had my hands full with a well-built colt who thought he was Bruce Lee. Crop must have figured his boys had it under control and signalled for three of them to break off and head through the rear entrance. I figured they'd probably take the side alley and ambush our boys out front. The Kung Fu kid was distracted for a moment as the Lieutenant who wasn't keeping Tank busy and two of his comrades flew past. I didn't miss the opportunity and took the kid out of the game with a haymaker before hurrying after them. Nobody followed me out.

The lane behind Hansel's place was just wide enough to reverse a refuse truck, but it looked like that hadn't happened in a long time. The place was strewn with rotting bags and dumpsters half filled with empty bottles and take-away cartons. A ten foot high chain link fence ran along the opposite perimeter and beyond lay the parking lot of a distribution depot. I called out to the Outriders who were already half way up the lane. I don't know why, just figured I could slow them up or something before they got out front and ambushed our boys. The two in front carried on running without breaking stride, but Crop's Lieutenant stopped and turned around to see who'd shouted him.

I expected him to come at me fast and furious, but he paused before walking back down the alley towards me like he was making his mind up about something. I stayed put and let him come on.

"You really want to dance with me, or shall we sit it out and talk like two old men who should know better?" he called to me.

I didn't know what to make of that. I was wary. Most likely it was a stall before getting close enough for a sucker punch, but I wasn't sure. I didn't answer him.

I let him come on until we were a few yards apart. He must have sensed I was getting twitchy and stopped just out of range.

"We came to parley with the Pistols, man, but seems your Tank was too full to listen," he chuckled at his own joke. "Came to tell you about the girl and what happened to her. Father Hancock's pretty sister, you know? Rachael?"

I didn't move, but hearing her name hurt me raw inside. What business had the Outriders to come and talk to us about her? I opened my mouth to speak, but nothing came out.

"We know what happened to her, man. We know how she died and who did it. It was a piece of work, man. Used ropes to tie her down." He made it sound like he'd wanted to give her some himself. He was visualising it. The way she would have struggled. The way she wouldn't have been able to stop him.

I didn't want to hear this. I didn't want to hear how she died. Why couldn't he just shut up? He sounded as though he was proud or something. Perhaps that was it. Perhaps the Outriders felt they'd got large enough no one could touch them if they admitted it was one of theirs who killed her.

"Used the same rope to strangle her, after. Scrrrruck!" He smiled like he expected me to understand. Empathise even.

The memory of her gentle, honest smile hung in my mind, the one beacon of hope I'd seen in so many years. It was too much. I couldn't hear anymore, but he was relentless.

"The guy who did it said he enjoyed himself. He was one of ours he..."

I don't remember taking the knife from the sheath strapped to my belt, and I don't know how I managed to cover the distance between us as fast as I did, but we found we were both looking down in shock to where my hunting knife was buried up to its hilt in his gut with my hand still gripping the handle. Our foreheads were almost touching and I could feel his breath on my face as we both watched the stain spread steadily on his shirt. The remains of a frenzied shout died away on the air before I realised it had come from my mouth only moments before. I looked into his face and repeated it, quiet this time. "I loved her," I said.

The strangest thing was he didn't slump to the floor clutching his stomach like they do in the movies. The way they try to staunch the flow to hold onto whatever life they have left. Instead, although his face began to show pain and confusion, I felt gentle hands take my elbows and move them towards him like he wanted me to make the knife go deeper. I resisted and tried to pull it out, but it wouldn't come. Maybe it had got twisted behind a rib or something, but it felt more like he was keeping it there somehow. Like he wouldn't let it go yet. Like it belonged to him now.

"I didn't know, man. I wouldn't have...", but he didn't finish the sentence. Just held my gaze like he understood now.

I could hear sirens heading into town from two directions, but whatever words he had left to say were important to him and I had no choice but to listen to them.

"The guy who done it was one of the new boys," he managed, "boasting all over. But we done him, man. Everybody loved the Father. We done him. Gone to the river."

A wave of nausea hit me as I realised they'd come to tell us it was all over and they'd dealt with it themselves. No more mistrust. No more hate. They'd come to parley. Maybe lay down turf boundaries. Start again. Why didn't we realise? Why had they come into Hansel's in numbers and risk a fight?

Blood was coming from his mouth now and his shirt and mine were soaked in the same red. I found I was supporting more and more of his weight on the hilt of my knife and helped him down to the ground as gently as I could. I wanted to tell him I understood now. I wanted to tell him I would do anything to undo what I'd done. Those words never came, but there was one thing I found I could give him.

"Name's Ariel," I said.

We stared at each other like men who had truly recognised another soul, only to have them snatched away in death at the same moment. The pain had gone from his eyes now, but a look came over him all concerned as the sirens got closer.

"What are you worth Ariel?" he asked. "What are you worth?"

He closed his eyes and went still. The knife came out easily. My brother didn't need it anymore.

***

I opened my eyes to find a girl of about twelve watching me warily through ginger bangs that swept untidily across her face. She was on the far side of a dirt road, sat on the top rung of a solid ranch fence. She swung her legs to and fro in the sunshine while she slowly chewed her gum.

I'd run out of gas somewhere south of Memphis on route seventy nine the previous evening and had simply pulled off onto the nearest dirt road to set up camp. My bike was propped against a tree nearby.

She kept on watching while I climbed out of the bed roll and started to fish in my gear for the primus. I smiled at her and went back to the business of making coffee.

While the water was heating she asked, "Where you from, mister?" she managed to say it without missing a beat in her chewing.

"All over," I answered noncommittally. "Where am I now? What's this place called?"

"Oh it ain't nowhere 'particular, mister." She jumped down from the railing apparently satisfied I was both harmless and of no further interest.

She was about to set off up the lane when she paused and asked, "You looking for harvest work? My Daddy's looking for hands about now. You want me to tell him you're here?"

I thought about it for a moment and breathed deeply. I guess I had to be somewhere, and this here nowhere was as far as I'd got. It was as good as any for now.

Strangers on a Train

Maithreyi Nandakumar

It was a stroke of good fortune that got us tickets on the crowded train that night. We were returning from Darjeeling via Siliguri to Calcutta. Our friends had told us to fill a whisky bottle with black tea to bribe the ticket inspector if we didn't get reservations but that hadn't been necessary.

I'd been to Darjeeling before with friends, towards the end of the Gorkhaland agitation – in 1987. Then, it had been lights out at six and dinner on the hotel room floor served by a wizened old man who'd brought us dal, chapattis and a meagre *subji* with hot ginger tea from his basement kitchen. Our guide who'd taken us in the Jeep had mysteriously vanished after dropping us back and we'd heard gunshots in the pitch black night from our bedroom. It made us giggle uncontrollably but we felt safe and slept rather well.

Three years later, I was there with you and imagined for some reason that this would be a more grown up experience. Already, we'd had to hitch a ride in an important looking official's car when our bus broke down on our way to the mountains. He asked us both to sit in front next to the driver. Thank goodness for good old Ambassadors with a wide two-seater sofa at the front and back. No fussy seatbelts back then. Darjeeling itself was damp and cold and the dreadlocked yaks in the mall quite smelly. I'd bragged to you about how exciting my previous trip had been, being close to real danger, until our own encounter with some slick strangers on our return journey.

You nudged me awake and pointed out that the sleeper berth had to come down so that passengers could resume sitting. I stared groggily at the front page news of the Bengali daily being read by the man in front – of the court appearance of a notorious killer and tried to make sense of it, not knowing the language. Men in their nightclothes were squeezing paste onto toothbrushes and were brushing their teeth as they stood in line for their turn at the sink. Some women were adjusting their saris back to their appropriate standards of modesty. Wet fields and multiple pylons flashed by after the earlier station and the train seemed re-energised for its final lap.

So, when the elegantly dressed man in a pristine white kurta and pressed pyjamas stood in front of me, I smiled and nodded politely, making nothing of it. I was more preoccupied with the mesmerising rhythm of the train's wheels that made me feel purposeful, filled with anticipation of what lay ahead. The stranger's left cheek bulged with his morning *paan* and his teeth and tongue were stained red. He ignored me and decided to speak to you, shaking your hand and smiled and said something in a dialect that neither of us could follow. We saw him do the same to all the others too. I looked at you with an unspoken question and you shrugged, your expression putting it down to the exaggerated courtesy common on such journeys.

I decided to tidy up around me and made sure all our stuff was put away into our suitcase. The train had just over an hour to go and the landscape outside had changed from the undulating idyllic rice fields to thatched huts and rundown buildings. We were nearing the big city. Suddenly, the red mouthed, slicked-back hair and trimmed moustache man came back, this time with a toolbox in hand, and told me in a curt voice to move aside. His friend did the same to you at the other end and we stood up hurriedly to get out of their way. The politeness of before was gone and they weren't interested in giving us an explanation.

They worked with efficient ease as they went about unscrewing the plywood panel under the window. They repeated the same to the right side of the compartment, their faces so serious that no one dared to interfere or demand answers. Out of the exposed cavities came polythene bags of children's toys in garish pink and red, flimsy Frisbees and tacky gadgets which were all emptied into the waiting holdall and packed away quickly. As they zipped their bags, the train drew up to the penultimate stop and they got out and merged into the mass of humanity, as ordinary as anyone else. We'd just witnessed a heist, albeit of modest ambitions.

Every now and again, when I'm sitting on the train from Paddington to Temple Meads, I remember that journey. I watch the bored faces of my fellow passengers when you call me from your car asking what we'll be having for dinner. I sigh, yearning momentarily for a little drama.

The Green Tin Box

Suzanna Stanbury

I haven't thought this deeply since Mum died. Five years ago cancer took Mum and now life is taking Granddad. He can't go yet – I still need him. For a quarter of my life he's been all I've got, and when he's gone I'll have no-one.

"Is that you, Saus?"

"Yes, Granddad. Shush now you need to conserve your energy."

"Why? If I'm going to meet the almighty I may as well make use of what energy I've got left." His words are punctuated by wheezes, croaks and chest-rattles.

Granddad appears lost in the narrow hospital bed, frail and withered, his body barely dents the bed-clothes. Hearing his voice, I can't help but smile. He's still Granddad. Sharp, acerbic and principled.

"Saus – listen. This is important."

"Ssh, Granddad. The nurse is looking. She told me you shouldn't be excited."

"I'm *not* excited. Come closer, I'm not up to shouting."

I lean in. He still has the same Granddad smell: machine grease; soft bay from hair oil and musky old man scent. Just for a second I wonder what I'll smell like when I'm his age.

"You know the green tin box."

Of course I know his green tin box. Every time Granddad opened the safe I would see it, and wonder what was inside. What riches had to be double hidden – first in the safe and then locked inside the box. When I was younger I tried many times to get into the safe, and always failed. Mum caught me once, twisting the dial with my ear to the door – just like they do in the films. She went crazy. Slapped my leg so hard I had red finger marks on my thigh for hours. I kept going into the bathroom and pulling down my jeans to check if the slap marks had gone. It was my mark of shame she said for trying to be a thief. But I wasn't a thief! I just wanted to look in the box. Everything else in the safe I could see whenever the heavy grey metal door swung open. The stack of money; piles of legal papers: envelopes; a big roll of deeds; all that sort of thing held no interest to me – except for the money, of course. It had the thrill of what it was. So much cash frightened me. It seemed unreal. The 50 pences and pound coins in my moneybox were what I recognised as money. This was adult money. And then there was the green tin box. On the front was a circular lock, with no key to be seen. I wondered if it had been tucked inside the stack of money.

Years later the box was still a mystery to me and now it appeared I was about to find out what was in it.

"The safe combination is 230532. The key to the green box is in the toe of my left Wellington boot – behind the sock." Typical Granddad, choosing a place I'm not likely to venture – let alone touch. The smell of the thick hiking socks he used to keep his wellie boots a snug fit haunts me. From time to time, Mum used to remove his 'Limberger' socks, as she used to call them, and wash them. But since she's been gone they've not been touched and the stink of cheese is increasingly evident whenever you open the boot-room door.

"There's a letter in the box. For you. Explaining." He wheezes out this last bit, it sounds so painful. His eyes close. He grimaces with the effort from just forming the words.

"Granddad, you shouldn't be talking, you're making yourself feel worse."

"What's worse than death?" Even through his wheezing he still tries to smile.

"Fate?"

"Good old Saus. Taught you well. Keep a smile on your face – do no wrong."

"I told you not to let him talk. It tires him."

I hadn't heard the nurse come up behind me. Her shoes are thick-soled and silent.

"Sorry."

She reaches over me, holds Granddad's wrist. "It won't be long now. Sit quietly. Call me when you need to."

And she's gone.

I sit staring at Granddad wondering what death looks likes. I never got to see Mum; at 15 years old they thought I was too young to be there at the end. Granddad said I should remember her as she was. Keep that image tucked safely away. Auntie Reba stayed with me. She flew over especially. Auntie Reba had fallen out with mum when she met Dad. She didn't approve of Dad. And it turned out, with good reason, as he left us when I was small. I barely remember him.

It hit me. Would Dad come back after Granddad died? I didn't like the thought and shoved it away into the darkness at the back of my mind.

The moment arrives in which Granddad leaves. His eyes are closed. He relaxes, sinks back into the bed as if his entire body is as weightless as a cloud. His skin softens, all the creases in his face seem to fade away to nothing. Reaching out to take his hand, it seems so delicate; I lower my face and kiss it before the warmth goes.

"Goodbye, Granddad. I'll never forget you, don't forget me wherever you go."

***

I go home. Sit in the chair in the living room until the furniture fades around me into that dusk; the dusk of the last day my granddad lived. My stomach rumbles so I go to the kitchen, take a block of cheese out of the fridge and cut off a chunk. There's bread left; stale with bits of blue mould growing like flowers. I cut those bits out just like Granddad taught me to do. "Don't waste food!" he always said. "You never know when you will next see any."

Mum used to tell him the war was long ago and food was plentiful now, there was enough good food to let the bad go to waste.

"Until the next time."

She never had an answer when he said that phrase.

I feel stronger after eating some food. In a trance I go into the boot room, ignore the stench of cheese – Limberger, just like Mum described it. I extract the key from Granddad's sock; take it to the safe, place it on the top. I take a deep breath and turn the dial. 230532. Three loud consecutive clicks herald the door opening. It swings wide, just as I had watched it do so many times before – the only difference being, this time *I* opened it.

Ignoring everything else inside, I take out the box; place it, almost reverentially on the desk, sit on the tan leather-backed chair and look at the box. I expect the key to be stiff; hard to turn. But it moves smoothly, the lock must be well oiled, well-used. Inside is an envelope. Thick cream-coloured paper with my name written exactly in the middle of the envelope. That was Granddad – so precise. *Saul Greensfelder.*

Bless him, he's put a seal on the flap. A slick of gold leaf, stamped with SG. His initials. My initials. Mum never married Dad. She was still Dara Greensfelder when she died. My parents had lived in sin. *Chet.* Auntie Reba called it. She hated dad, and most likely still does.

I don't want to break the seal. Because Granddad made it. Perhaps I could slit along the top of the envelope? On the desk is a marble desk tidy, with places for pens, ink pots and... A silver letter opener with a snake twisted around the orbed top. Taking a deep breath I insert the opener and pull upwards. The paper is thick; it wants to stay in one piece. But finally the envelope opens. Inside is a wad of writing paper, unlined; covered in Granddad's small neat handwriting in the dark brown ink he always liked to use.

Dear Saus,

This letter is agony to write. My soul aches having to tell you all this, my dearest grandson, Sausage – remember how you got that name: when you swiped all the bratwurst from the plate when you were little.

Dear Saus, I wish you could have known my father. He was a wonderful man. I idolised him. A renowned silversmith in Bavaria, he was sought out by the great, the good... and others. Whenever a keepsake was required they called upon my father to create something beautiful. I didn't usually go with my father when he delivered items to his clients, but this time was different. We went to a place on the Obersalzberg, a pale house. It seemed vast. I was only six years old. I stayed behind my father, slight, a blink of humanity – the men who showed my father into the office considered me too insignificant to notice me.

My father put the parcel on the desk, stepped back to observe what its new owner would do. The paper was torn away, the box opened, revealling a silver inkstand – an eagle cupping ink pots in the curl of its magnificent wings. Exclamations were made over the fine workmanship, the intricate detail of the engraving – when he was making the inkstand my father had explained to me it had been commissioned to mark a political victory.

I was standing by the door, holding onto an ornate chair with a jacket hanging over the back, the mouldings of the chair made the shoulders of the jacket appear as if a hunchback was inside; a monster.

The man's face mesmerized me. He stared for many minutes at the inkstand, scrutinising every inch of it. Finally he placed it on the desk and looked at my father. The man looked tired, his eyes bulged, and I thought perhaps his left eye had a slight turn in it. And then he twitched his lip.

"Thank you for the gift. You can go."

I saw my father stiffen. It had been a commission – worth a lot of money. The night before I overheard him telling my mother how worried he was – this had happened too many times before – items ordered and then not paid for, accepted as a gift when they had not been. And each time my father lost money, more and more money. He had risked everything for this one final commission – the last hope to save his business.

I wasn't thinking. I was so angry for my father. It wasn't right. My hand slipped into the jacket's pocket and pulled something out. I secreted it away in my clothing.

My father didn't move. I wasn't the only one who could sense his disquietude. The turn in the man's eye worsened, my skin froze as his gaze darkened. I couldn't understand his expression. Realising my father was leaving I hurried after him out of the room.

We returned home to find a letter had arrived. In his desperation my father had written to his old friend Len Winterstein asking for advice. Len, an astute man with an

English wife, sensing the troubles to come in Europe had moved his business to his wife's home town in the north west of England. Len said he could offer no advice but my father could save both their businesses by them working together. It transpired Len had been involved in a furnace accident the year before and the surgeon had been unable to save one of his hands. The letter enclosed three open passage tickets.

My father did not need to dwell upon Len's offer. My parents packed what we needed most from our belongings and we set out for the next train. As the bus pulled away I was looking out of the back window, and saw a car pull up outside our shop. When four men in uniform leapt out and hammered on the shop door I knew they had come for me.

The item I had stolen was a pen. I was ashamed and yet proud of what I had done. During the journey to England I concealed it carefully in the lining of my coat. After what I had seen that day I knew the pen must always remain hidden.

I kept the pen with me at all times, hiding it carefully. It wasn't until I had grown up and obtained my own home the pen found its place in the green tin box.

And now, dearest Saus, the pen is yours. Be careful with it. You are a sensible boy; I think you will know what to do.

All the love in the world,

Granddad xxx

I put down the letter, pull the box towards me and lift a sheet of lined blue notepaper. Underneath is a roll of linen cloth. I take it out and slowly unroll it, revealing the pen. It's thick-barrelled and when I lift it and feel its weight, I know at once it is made of solid gold. The pen rests in my palm like lead. Slowly, I turn it. A smooth polished panel bears an inscription, *A.H.*

I put the pen back in the box under the blue paper, close and lock the lid. And then I return it to the safe.

Jago Comes To Dinner

AA Abbott

"Don't do this," Jago says. "You'll regret it."

You laugh, scornfully. "Does it look like it?" you say. Then you smile, and take a scalpel, and slice into his cheek, just a little bit.

"There," you purr. "No regrets."

Blood oozes from the wound. Crimson droplets splash onto Jago's black cashmere jumper, moist circles catching the light from your chandelier. He screams.

Like a remorseless amoeba, the city has engulfed much of the green belt around it, but not your smallholding. Your fields are empty of human souls, livestock sleeping now dusk has fallen. It's snowing outside the farmhouse, the fairies' white cloak enhancing night's silence. Within, there is only the tick of the clock and the crackle of the log fire. And the screams that no man but you will hear.

You staunch the blood with a cottonwool bud soaked in alcohol. "This might sting," you murmur. Although, by the looks of it, not as much as his eyes, which are puffy and bruised already. You were tempted to punch his jaw, but didn't want to break it. At least, not yet. You don't want to make it harder for him to talk.

Jago is sweating. A bead of perspiration trickles down his lightly tanned neck, mingling with his cologne. It smells expensive. He must fancy himself with the girls. You imagine him driving a young woman in an F-type Jaguar convertible, wind streaming through their hair. She's turning an adoring gaze on him. As the fleeting thought begins to solidify, you feel rage take command of you. There's a bowl of nuts on the table: walnuts, hazels, Brazils. You pick up the nutcracker.

"Anything you'd like to tell me?" you say.

He squirms and moans. You unzip his jeans and apply the nutcrackers; a light squeeze to begin with, then enough force to close the pincers fully before removing them. He thrashes around in his chair; your chair, the solid oak dining chair to which you've tied him securely with thick rope, using techniques learned from the Boy Scouts many years ago. The chair rocks without tipping over. You wouldn't care if it did. This time, his scream is one of despair, a shrill wail swiftly muffled as he starts to retch.

"Where's my car?" you say.

Jago sobs. Tears fall from his long-lashed, swollen eyes. "I'll get it, Doc," he offers, his voice trembling with pain. "Let me out of here, and I'll fetch it."

Does he think you were born yesterday? "No," you say coldly. "Give me the keys. Tell me where I can find it." You hold the nutcrackers an inch from his groin.

"Gone," he gasps, "it's gone."

You throw the nutcrackers to the floor, gaining momentary satisfaction from the discordant crash and bounce as they hit the boards. "I know it's gone," you say, exaggerating each word. "I want to know where."

He slumps into a sullen heap. You slap the uncut cheek. "Where?" you yell.

It seems a lifetime since you first rang him, off to a medical conference and unwilling to pay for airport parking. Jago was more talkative then, questioning you about your research and your conference as he drove you to the airport. He would clean the car, he promised, garage it and collect you on your return. Except he wasn't there to meet you at all. You returned with suitcases, jetlag, a bottle of duty-free whisky for the keen young valet. You waited at the airport for hours, phoning his mobile repeatedly, hearing a brief recorded message, leaving voicemails for him, frustrated when the calls weren't returned. Finally, you took a taxi and spent a sleepless night worrying about your car, the new Jaguar that was the culmination of a lifetime's savings and dreams. Not just worrying, though, but plotting to secure its safe return.

Defiance flickers in Jago's eyes. "I'll tell the police," he threatens.

"Like that's going to happen," you taunt him. "Anyway, why should they believe the word of a car thief?"

"Prove it."

"I have proof enough. I had a car, a new silver Jag, and it's disappeared."

"Can't prove I took it," he repeats. "Anyway, what's the big deal? Insurance paid out, didn't it? You're driving a Merc now." He spits the words out. "Victimless crime, innit."

"How many times must I say it, Jago? There is no Mercedes. I have no daughter." You laugh without mirth. "I asked myself, what will it take to lure Jago back here?"

You'd planned it carefully. For weeks, months even, you rang every mobile number promising a drive-away cleaning service in the city. You knew Jago would have acquired another phone. It was obvious once his number became unobtainable. To encourage him, you called on your throwaway PAYG Nokia, using your new identity. Jago liked his dirty talk with young blonde Tia. Anything's possible, with the help of voice software and pictures downloaded from Facebook.

You reeled him in surely, like a fish hooked on your bait: promising Jago your ripe female body and your curmudgeonly father's new Mercedes.

Wheels are turning in Jago's cunning, but barely educated, brain. "It was a trick," he says, his expression crestfallen.

Your face darkens and you cut to the chase. "I'm through with playing nice," you tell him. "I want my car."

Jago giggles hysterically. You stroll to the fire, and prod the sizzling logs with a poker. It glows red. You wave it meaningfully at the car thief. "Start talking," you say.

"No!" Jago screams. The stench rising from him makes you gag. It's more than sweat. You really don't want to be close to him.

"Well?"

"Listen, Doc," Jago sobs, "that car's gone for good, broken up, innit? Gears and engine to Abu Dhabi, rest of it to the scrap heap." He shrinks as you advance with the red-hot poker. "I'll get you another one," he shrieks desperately. "Audi, Range Rover, any car you want. They're all parked up on drives in the city, just waiting for me to take them. Mostly, I don't need to get the keys, see? Use my laptop, and I can drive a car away, get the paperwork legit and you'll have it next week." He attempts an ingratiating smile

You replace the poker by the fireside. "Let me think," you say.

Jago looks hopeful, little realising you'd never take up his offer. You'll tell the police about your vanishing car, file the insurance claim and dispose of this smelly excuse for a man.

"I've made up my mind," you say conversationally. "I'm afraid you made a mistake when you called me Doc. If I were a doctor, I'd have taken the Hippocratic oath, but I'm not, and I haven't."

He looks blank. The lowlife has no idea what you're talking about, or of its significance for him. You put him right.

"The Hippocratic oath would bind me to preserve human life, Jago. But actually, I'm a vet, a researcher and a part-time farmer. I'm under no such obligation."

You had considered keeping him at the farm for experiments. But he'd be too much trouble. He can't even keep his pants clean.

"Goodbye, Jago," you say, and administer more chloroform, as you did when he entered the farmhouse.

You can easily carry him over your shoulder to the pigsty, your feet crunching virgin snow. It isn't slippery yet. Later, there will be ice and the roads will be impassable. Jago had mentioned Range Rovers. Only a fool would accept his offer to steal one in the city, a city to which he will never now return,

174

but perhaps you should buy one with the insurance money. Yet, although in other matters you are ruled by logic, a car is for you an affair of the heart.

Snowflakes melt on your skin as they fall. They're melting onto Jago too, but he doesn't wake.

The big freeze has reduced the whiff of the piggery. You wouldn't know animals lived there until you open the door. Even so, Jago smells worse. The half dozen pigs inside, all rare breeds, scan you both once you switch on the light. You've made them wait, and they're hungry. You wink at them. "Dinnertime," you shout.

The Longhouse

Judy Darley

The dream never alters in its intensity though the details change. I wake up in the house where I grew up, and have a sense that something is terribly wrong. I slip out of bed, creak out on to the landing. The house is empty but for slanting shadows, fragments of light that flick past, disappear. I go into every room in turn, but each is empty. I step into the kitchen,

and it's there that I find the shrunken head I brought back with me from Borneo, grinning at me from the windowsill. I pick it up, cradle it in my hands, and I think I hear it croon my name.

***

"Excuse me, do you know where this bus goes?"

I look up. Tourists. They always target me, because I'm fair-skinned, tall, so obviously not local. To them I must resemble a life-ring in a dark and unfamiliar sea.

"Where're you trying to get to?" I ask.

The man, face flecked with greying stubble, pulls out a crumpled leaflet advertising a beach hotel. The photo shows a pristine white shore. They must have got a shock when they saw the litter that washes up each day, refuse from the refugee camp set a few kilometres up the coast.

"Yes, this is the right bus," I say. "The driver will be along soon, ten minutes or so."

The woman leans forward, her face avid with interest. "You live here? In Kota Kinabalu?"

I try to guess which answer will make most sense to her. She reminds me of my mum, is probably just as incapable of guessing the ages of 'young people'. "Gap year," I say, and paste on a smile.

"How lovely!" she exclaims, but the man looks puzzled, indicates my left hand.

"You're wearing a wedding ring."

I've forgotten to take it off. Careless. "Makes life easier when you're travelling alone," I improvise.

"Gosh, must be difficult," the woman says.

"Sometimes. I meet people, though," I say. "Like you."

That makes her smile, helps her believe we're friends. I glance at her husband. He's watching a man passing with a trolley laden with cages; white mice, gerbils, guinea pigs – all piled up.

"Dinner, I suppose," he says, amused, and I feel a pinch of anger.

"Pets, actually," I tell him. "Just like in England."

I pretend to check the timetable. "Listen, it's another twenty minutes till the bus goes, and it takes quite a windy route – at least an hour to the hotel. With three of us a taxi will cost about the same."

"I thought you said ten minutes," the man says, but the woman is already nodding enthusiastically.

"What a good idea. Where are you staying?"

"At a hostel near your hotel. Look, there's a taxi."

I lead the way to where Miko leans against his cab, pretending not to eavesdrop. "Hello Madams, Sir." He smiles broadly as he opens the door to the backseat. "Where to go?"

The woman slides in. The man hesitates though. "I prefer to sit in front. My legs are long and…"

"I get carsick if I sit in the back," I say quickly. "I'll scooch the seat forward so you'll have plenty of room."

"Let her sit in front if she wants to, George," the woman says. "I'm Viv, love, what's your name?"

"Becky," I say. I'm never quite sure why I lie at this point, but somehow it feels better this way, makes me feel less implicated. "Nice to meet you."

George grimaces, folds himself into the backseat, puffing irritably.

We set off. I pretend to give Miko directions and we exchange a few words of Malay mixed in with Miko's tribal dialect.

"Gosh, you're fluent!" Viv exclaims.

"I love languages," I turn in my seat to tell her. I think I glimpse a promising dapple of envy in her eyes. "It's one of the fun things about travelling, isn't it? Listen, the driver's asked if we'd like to see the longhouse where he lives – it's just near here. What do you think?"

Viv's eyes light up but George grunts. "We already saw some at the Sabah Museum."

"But this is a real one, lived in by families with children and chickens and goats…"

"Don't mention the guinea pigs," Miko mutters in Malay and I pretend to be delighted.

"He says his grandma and the other ladies would love to show you their beading. And they have some local rice wine we can try."

"Oh, George, an authentic longhouse! Wouldn't that be interesting? We'll have so much to tell Larry!" Viv turns her attention back to me. "Larry's our son – he's studying Anthropology. Borneo is just his kind of place!"

George glowers. He looks hot, pressed up in the backseat.

"Seal the deal," Miko says to me in Malay. I nod, smile.

"Did you see the headhunting exhibit at the museum?" I ask, directing my question purposefully at George. "Gave me the shivers! The driver says his family are part of some tribe that's a sub-group of the Kadazan-Dusuns." I make a show of struggling with the pronunciation. "Weren't they headhunters?"

"More than a century ago, perhaps," George snaps, but I can tell he's finally intrigued. "No harm in a detour, I suppose."

I say a few words to Miko and he shouts out: "Good, very good!" He picks up his mobile phone to warn the families we're on our way.

When we arrive, no one's around apart from a few half-naked children, stripped of their jeans moments earlier by their parents. They're playing at being warriors, smacking long sticks together with gusto. Funny, Miko told me once that when he was young that's just how he was, except for him the half-nudity was a fact of everyday life rather than a manipulation. Our own kids are tucked away out of sight, their milkiness a dead giveaway even if neither forgets their role and runs up to hug me.

We pile out of the taxi. I can see the intrigue on both their faces. Miko yells to the children: "Run ahead, make sure everyone is ready."

He mutters to me and I tell George and Viv to remove their shoes before entering the longhouse. Viv slips out of her sandals and follows Miko quickly up the struts of the bamboo ladder. I wait while George slowly unlaces his heavy hiking boots, hearing Viv's happy squeaks above us.

Maria is in position, boobs out, feeding six-month-old Trevor. Just behind her, Rachel and Caroline are working on beaded sandangs. Miko calls to me: "Tell them about the stories, see if we can sell a couple." He picks up one Caroline finished previously, pointing to motifs. "Say this is the tale of a warrior vying to win the heart of the woman he loves."

I relay the story and Viv is entranced. "Oh Becky, is it for sale? George, can we buy it?"

He snorts, unimpressed, but hands over the notes.

I spot the camera hanging from his neck. "I'm sure they won't mind if you take photos."

He shrugs, but starts snapping away. The sound of the clicking is the cue for the children to dart in, start playing picturesquely with wooden, tin and bamboo toys. Anything plastic has been shut away in their rooms. They climb up and over the mountainous sacks of rice that sit outside each door, giggling and posing for George's lens.

"Are the toys made by the tribe?" Viv asks.

I shoot Miko a glance.

"John bought some from the market yesterday," he says in Malay. "I'll get them."

He wanders off, returns with a selection he lays out on the floor. Viv crouches down to see them. "Oh, aren't they lovely?"

They're little more than trash refashioned into rudimentary animals, but she buys two jagged crocodiles. "We're hoping to see real ones in the Kinbatangan River," she tells one of the children. He opens his mouth to respond, sees me shake my head, closes it fast.

George turns from his photography, sees Viv popping the crocs into her bag. "What did you get those for, Viv? It's not like we're got grandkids to give them to."

"Not yet, my love, but Larry…"

"Larry's not ready for all that nonsense yet, you silly…"

"You don't know that!" Viv exclaims. I have the impression this is a long-disputed point. "All it'll take is for him to meet the right girl, like lovely Becky here." She turns to me. "Larry would just adore you!"

George looks so sceptical that I'm embarrassed.

John approaches carrying a bottle of rice wine. Maybe that'll help. Miko ushers us to sit down, hands us each a tumbler full. He drinks his own, smacks his lips. I sip mine, try not to cough. It's rough stuff, worse even than last week's.

Viv sips daintily and chokes. "Bit strong for me, I'm afraid."

"Me too," I say thankfully.

"All the more for me then, eh?" George brightens up at last.

As he works his way through the bottle, I steer the conversation round to headhunting, and Miko dictates gruesome things for me to tell them. By the time John returns with the tray of 'shrunken heads' it's almost too easy.

"Gosh, look at the way their jaws protrude!" Viv comments.

"Guess that's down to the way the brains are extracted," I suggest uneasily. The fur has been burnt off, but if they look too closely, there's a chance they'll notice the resemblance to a beloved family pet. I point to the one on the end. "Miko says this one was a matter of honour – the head was severed while he was still in battle. Imagine that, thwack!" I shudder extravagantly and Viv follows suit.

"Larry would just adore one of these," she tells me, in the same tone she used when saying how much her son would adore me.

Miko grins at me over George's shoulder. "Tell them the heads are talismans," he says. "Tell them, the more the better to bring good fortune to their home."

I shake my head slightly – it's not good to get greedy. I pretend to buy one, slip it into my bag, watch them buy one for themselves, another for their son.

And that's that – a good day's work. We pile back into the taxi and drive along the coast road. Miko drops me off in front of a hostel, swooping back to pick me up once he's deposited George and Viv. As I climb into the car he kisses me hard on the lips. "You devious angel," he crows, and we drive home to the longhouse.

That night I have the first of the dreams that will lead to our break up. I wake in my childhood bedroom, only somehow it's also our room in the longhouse. Miko is snoring beside me, our children asleep between us. I hear someone calling out in the darkness: "Becky, Becky!" The sound comes from my bag. I slip out of bed, unzip the bag, find the shrunken head inside. Only now it isn't a cavy head with all its fur burnt off, but a genuine shrunken head, with a small, wizened version of Viv's trusting face.

No Rest for the Wicked

Maithreyi Nandakumar

I turn to lie more comfortably on this tree trunk. I could be a movie star in a dream scene. My diaphanous white sari is draped over the dense leaves. In the neighbouring branches, restless winged creatures fuss around their little ones. You can spot the cheating cuckoos that use other birds' nests, the boring crows and the parakeets that are exactly the colour of the leaves of this *neem* tree. I find their activity quite annoying – it spoils my moment of languorous indulgence. Just as I'm about to enter the zone of some serenity, I hear the chanting below.

The fools have returned to pray. The anthill at the base of the trunk is a shrine of fear and faith – in honour of its squatter-in-chief, the King Cobra. On and on they go, praying to Shiva's favourite pet, for the happy marriage of their daughters. I could tell those shrinking virgins a thing or two about wedded bliss, if they bothered to ask me.

My thoughts are rudely interrupted by some loud wailing. Just listening to that shrieking makes me want to take a graceful leap and fall into the cavernous well that's just behind – to drown into oblivion. I've tried to walk down its curving steps, slippery with moss but get too frightened before the final step and clamber back. When I do try it, for a few moments, I feel like a beautiful princess, anklets on my feet, holding my skirt up gracefully, to just below my knees – with the right expression of knowing innocence.

The rains have made the area around the anthill soggy – and the shallow bowls of milk will turn sour if the raving devotees don't hurry up and leave. I could do with some nourishment – forget the lazy reptile. Behind me is the outhouse not far from the well – I can't bear to look at that cesspit of malevolence and utter shame.

No rest for the wicked, isn't that what they say? What's all the fuss about, you may wonder. In a way, it was quite satisfying to see the princess's family from the house opposite reduced to this, even if they don't really deserve what I did to them. Last night, I saw the slender beauty, sleepless at her window, desperate to slake her lust with a dream lover. The sight of all that yearning and pining curdled my stomach and I wanted to retch. I decided to play with her – games to tease, to titillate, to scare the living daylights out of her. I left her screaming for her mother.

I wish someone had heard my silent screams before I decided to wring the life out of my rather scrawny neck. The outhouse is hidden from my vision – beneath the dark green leaves of the mango tree. For a while now, that tree has stopped bearing fruit. I'd like to think in shocked reaction to what it witnessed that night.

I will never know the impact my death had on those two boorish brothers. I was married to the third one. The entire family has since moved away. The small one-roomed hut has been razed to the ground. The two elderly parents still work as cooks at the big house that belongs to a newspaper publisher – I see them walk by, looking rather pious. But when I arrived after our wedding, we all lived under one tiny roof. The older siblings and their wives had babies and toddlers sprawling everywhere. I was told that they took turns to use the shed in the garden when they needed 'privacy'. I can still remember the crazy sister-in-law who had come to visit. She who laughed at me from the day I joined this family. I was revolted by the way she dragged her husband into that smelly shack to demonstrate how it was done – all wink, wink, nudge, nudge before and after.

The last memory I have is of my cuckolded husband crying like a baby when they pulled me in after they'd had their fill of their own women. I can smell the stale breath of alcohol as they exhaled into my terrified face, my throat unable to scream. How could I even look at the hypocritical in-laws who would expect me to keep quiet? When they left me huddled in a corner, I took the decision to end it all. That story was hushed up – they continued to live here wearing pious expressions. They may be poor but they were "respectable".

And so, I listen to the prayers told to appease the evil spirit that resides in this tree. I laugh to myself at the respect I command in this halfway place – somewhere between death and re-incarnation.

Years later, the toxic life that existed in this secret woodland came to an effective end. They brought the tree down and dug up the dense vegetation, closed the well, knocked down the flimsy walls of the mud huts and flattened down the soil to make good. To pour concrete and neaten it into a flat, monotonous car park.

The wailing is relentless – the prospective suitor's family came to see the fragrant beauty for a suitable match but left in a hurry. Those jasmine cheeks had lost their colour after the visit I paid her last night – the doe eyes were too dull and lifeless. "She looked as if a ghost had thrashed her," they said. I let out a scream of amusement and sit up. There's no rest for the wicked.

Orchard End

Suzanna Stanbury

Why, oh why am I doing this on a rare day off. My car draws in at the back of a line of motorists hanging out of their car windows. Our frustration is palpable. A woman running in frantic circles is trying to catch a panicking llama. I leave the car to intervene.

"Police. Is it your llama, madam? A runaway llama! Any idea where it ran from?"

***

"Cassie! You're late." Auntie Dee bounds out of the front door the moment I pull up outside the bungalow. Of all the frivolous things I could be doing today, helping my Auntie Dee with the St Mary's Mound Bring and Buy Sale is not high on the list – even behind catching cavorting camelids.

"Escaped llama on the Tickenham Road – don't ask."

Auntie Dee's eyebrows rise up her forehead, but she remains undaunted by my deep sigh and weary expression.

"I won't. It's good you've had an animal encounter this morning, Cassie, as I've put you on the White Elephant stall. Come along, this way."

"Oh, goody, I love other people's unwanted Christmas presents."

"Now, now, don't be like that… you'll enjoy it." She chivvies me behind a table next to the coat-rack, then promptly vanishes. I stand there watching a motley assortment of church-going devotees filing in through the front door, straight past me and my stand full of bric-a-brac. There's a man selling wood-turned crafts on a pasting table by the under-stairs loo. He gives me a little wave, a grin, accompanied by a shrug of camaraderie, then returns to straightening a row of polished maple barometers.

Auntie Dee reappears. "This is Eleanor." She inclines her head towards the woman by her side. "Eleanor was kind enough to let us hold the sale at her bungalow after St Mary's went up in smoke, isn't that right, dear?"

Eleanor is one of those sixtyish women for whom youth dies screaming. Her blonde hair is neatly fastened in a chignon I can only describe as a work of art. All swooping swirls with nary a pin in sight, she reviews my short dark hair with an inscrutable expression. Eleanor's make-up is discrete and immaculate, and no doubt took about an hour to achieve. Her style of dress is far too trendy for her age. "He…llo." I spot her blue suede platform trainers, the sight of them catching my voice mid-word.

"Good morning, Cassie." Eleanor has a well-veneered tone. "I simply can't believe Dee set you to work and didn't let you have a cup of tea first. Dee! Take over the elephant until we get back. This way, Cassie."

The living room, a huge space with a deep curtain-less bay at the front and a long window overlooking verdant gardens to the side, is bustling with aged people bearing plates and cups. Three women are squashed behind a trestle table by the wall, wielding coffee pots, tea pots and cutting cakes as the queue wends its way along the plastic table cloth.

"Cassie! Do you see the brick wall at the edge of the lawn?" Pointing, Eleanor almost pokes a squat woman in a heather-coloured twin-set in the eye. "Behind it used to be the most beautiful orchard. No sooner did Mrs Monkshaft die, than developers snapped-up her land like that." The clip of her fingers next to my ear is like a bone snapping. "Awful! No respect, that sort of person. They couldn't get the planning permission through fast enough."

Letting out a wistful sigh, she toys with the single rope of pearls gleaming at her unlined throat. "Mrs Monkshaft was kind enough let my husband Gerald and I use the orchard. We often went in just for a walk about." Sighing again, she pats her immaculate hair and continues. "There were always pigs snuffling round the trees. Pigs and orchards go together. When a pig dies it's buried under an apple tree so it can nourish the root system. It is so important to follow tradition, don't you think so? Cassie?"

Unable to think of a suitable reply I'm grateful to a group of noisy pigeons that appear outside the bay, flapping and cooing before heading into the guttering, tail feathers dipping as they settle in. My gaze fixes on the warm red bricks of the garden wall and the narrow wooden gate set into it. I can almost picture the orchard that, until recently lay beyond: apples fermenting on the ground, drunken pigs scoffing, then snoring off their hangovers. An unattractive line of brown fencing towers above the old wall bordering the gardens of a small housing estate. I expect the orchard wall was listed and the developers couldn't touch it.

"I can still see apple trees at the far end."

"You *are* observant, Cassie," Eleanor smiles like a grass snake in the sun. "Yes… six ghastly commuter homes. Luckily for me, as you noticed… they kept the apple trees at the end of the orchard – one for each silly little garden. Each of them is about the size of a picnic blanket. Pointless!" she snorts.

"Did St Mary's really burn down?" I hold my rose patterned cup under an enormous quivering aluminium tea-pot a woman with tight curly hair is struggling to hold aloft.

"Did Dee tell you that?" snaps Eleanor. "Your aunt is *so* prone to exaggeration. It was a small fire under the stage in the church hall. We'd had a curate exchange with Santa Maria della Porto." Seeing my expression she smirks. "Milano. We got *their* Carlo in exchange for *our* Colin. Young Carlo thought gasping on his Consulate under the stage would be a good idea. In a confined space next to the nativity crib full of straw, I ask you. No sense, these Italian boys."

"Er..." I gesture towards a line of dining chairs set out against the flowered wallpaper where four nuns perch sipping tea. The fifth nun has her hand up her habit and a huge grin slathered across her face.

"Sister Winifred!" Shoving her cup at me, Eleanor runs nunward-bound. "What have I told you about doing that. Stop it at once! Come on, straight to the cloakroom. Oh, for goodness sake – don't touch the paintwork!"

The lady with the tea pot removes Eleanor's cup from my hand. "Poor Sister Winnie," she says, pursing her lips so they are as tight as her perm. She sloshes the dregs of the cup into a glass jug. "She's got a swift's nest where sense used to be." Tutting, she taps her iron grey hair with a gnarled finger.

Returning to the White Elephant stall, I find Auntie Dee enmeshed in conversation with a priest.

"Cassie!" Auntie Dee trills. "Here you are at last. Say hello to Father Barnabas."

"Barney, please." The priest beams at me. He has attractive blue eyes, with long dark lashes. I suspect mascara. "What on earth was up with Sister Winifred?" he asks, examining his fingernails. "I saw Eleanor rushing her into the downstairs loo as fast as two blackbirds darting over a hedge."

"Sister Winifred was… " Struggling for a suitable description under the questioning gaze of the effete clergyman, I incline my head sideways with a jerking motion while fluttering my hand.

"Oh, good golly Miss Molly. Not again. I thought we'd cured her of that unfortunate… urge." His manicure forgotten, his hand flies to his collar, fretting at it. I'm fighting back a smile.

"Not enough medication today, I suspect." Auntie Dee extracts herself from behind the table. "I *must* get a cup of coffee. Will you be joining me, Father?"

"I rather thought I may stay and have a chitty-chat with your niece." Having recovered his sensibilities, Father Barney gives me a wry smile. Oh, god I hope he's not going to tell me off for miming onanism. Instead he plucks from the table a pretty basket with a blue handle, turns it around a few times, lifts the lid for a sniff. "Lavender, gone-off." Discarding the basket, he wiggles his nose, presumably to chase out the remaining odour within. "Eleanor's been *so* generous allowing us to use her bungalow," he says. "It's the first time we've been allowed

194

in since Gerald… went." His eyelashes flutter. "It must have been incredibly difficult for her seeing the orchard destroyed last year. We *all* know it meant *so* much to her and Gerald. Eleanor was *devoted* to Gerald. Never saw them apart when he was home, and he wasn't home often if you know what I mean." He bats his eyelashes at me.

What a gossiper! "How old was Gerald when he died?"

Closing his eyes, Father Barney winces. "Not dead, Cassie. I rather suspect Gerald… legged-it." Chuckling as he adjusts his shirt-front Father Barney continues: "I don't use that phrase lightly, as there was talk Gerald was getting… over-fond of the chiropodist on Edward Road. Hark at me, I mustn't gossip."

A loud cough behind Father Chitty-Chat's head quells the unfortunate quip on the way out of my mouth. Executing a neat spin on the spot he reddens slightly. "Sister Scholastica!" he exclaims to the taller of two nuns. "I'm *so* glad you made it."

"I've brought Sister Anne Ascensión with me," the nun says in a voice so deep I wonder if Bryn Terfel in full habit has come round to see if he could pick up a few cheap pillow cases. "She's learning fund-raising. We've had some problems with frivolous distribution recently, haven't we, Sister?"

The smaller nun, spying the lavender basket, picks it up and holds it out. "How much is this?" she asks in a voice with a slight Irish lilt.

"Put it *down!*"

"Now, now, Sister, this is a confined space." Tempting them with talk of tea, Father Barney leads the two dark-draped figures away.

Thank goodness. Perhaps I'll get five seconds peace, before the next suburban drama erupts. A small bronze angel on the table takes my attention. Examining the angel, I find it engraved on the base: *'To my darling Gerald. Forever We Stay Strong'*.

Crikey. The tattling cleric was right – Eleanor *was* devoted. I pick up a carriage clock next – also engraved: *'To Gerald. Good luck on your retirement. Failand Pharmaceutical Supplies is missing you already'*. Hmm. So Gerald was a sales rep, was he? I wonder if the coquette of the cornpads was one of his customers? I wonder if he...?

"Cassie!" Auntie Dee's back. Bringing with her an elderly lady so stooped she has to turn sideways to look up at me. "Fliss wanted to say hello as she looked after you once when you were a baby."

"You was sick on me," says Fliss. "All down my cardigan it went. You don't do that now, do you?"

"Er... no. I'm usually contained nowadays, stomach-wise. Auntie Dee... This angel – look it says: 'From Eleanor to Gerald' – see the engraving?"

Taking the angel, Auntie Dee gives it the once over. "I've never seen that before," she sniffs.

"There's more of 'em down 'ere," says Fliss pointing under the table. "In a box, they is. I can see 'em."

I toe the box out. Many angels are crammed wing-to-wing in neat lines. All are different. Removing a handful for a closer look, suddenly my brain clicks into action.

"Wedding anniversaries!" I exclaim. "They're for wedding anniversaries." Auntie Dee... How long were Eleanor and Gerald married?"

"40 years." She's scrutinising an angel crafted in Royal Worcester china.

"40 years is ruby," says Fliss. "They'll be a red 'un in there somewhere."

I get down on my hands and knees, rummaging about in the box. "No red angel that I can see."

"Maybe Gerald didn't get past his 40th, if you get my gist," says Fliss. "But I don't like to cast no aspersions like."

"What do you mean?" Bending down like a heron at a pond, Auntie Dee attempts to look Fliss in the eye. "Of course he did – I went to their anniversary party!"

"I lives over the back of those matchbox 'ouses," Fliss says. "I don't 'spect you remembers my 'ouse, do you young Cassie, that time you came over and was sick on I?"

"Not if I was only a baby, no. Why do you ask?"

"My 'ouse is a tall 'un and I sees things. Well... I used to, before I got this crook-back of mine, now I just sees their shoes. But there was a time when I could see right into that old orchard of Molly Monkshaft's. Gerald and Eleanor used to go at it like the clappers of a summer's night when they knew old Molly was fast asleep. He liked a bit of rumpy pumpy did Gerald. He liked a bit full-stop, the randy old boar."

Looking embarrassed, Auntie Dee straightens up, rubbing her spine. "And you saw them, did you, Fliss?"

"I saw other things as well. Let's just say... those apple trees is doing well in the new gardens, aint they? Particularly the one at the end."

An eerie feeling makes me look towards the doorway. Eleanor's watching us, her blue eyes narrowed and flinty. The look on her face is frightening. It's a jolly good job Fliss can't see her or it would most likely have shocked the poor old dear to death. I've seen that look before. Normal people don't wear it. Dead pigs nourishing the roots! Of course.

"Eleanor!"

She zooms off. Tearing out from behind the table, I trip over the box of angels. Swiftly recovering my step, I run after Eleanor as she sprints through the kitchen, sending nuns scattering, heading out into the garden, across the lawn she comes to an abrupt halt. In her panic, Eleanor's forgotten the gate in the wall goes nowhere.

A Hint of Crime

Credits

Cover Image by Carolyn Stubbs – Copyright Carolyn Stubbs ©2015

Elizabeth 'Liz' Ascott photograph still from video Copyright Suzanne H Ferris ©2016

D A Allen photograph still from video Copyright Suzanne H Ferris ©2016

Flight 6051 by D A Allen – photograph, Copyright Judy Darley ©2016, titivated by Joe Beasant

The Beast by Liz Ascott – photograph, Copyright Joe Beasant ©2016

Flyleaf by Judy Darley – photograph, Copyright Judy Darley ©2016

The Convenience Store – by Richard M S Kemp photograph, Copyright Richard M S Kemp © 2016

Snip by Tim Kindberg, photograph, Copyright Tim Kindberg ©2016

Springtime by Maithreyi Nandakumar, photograph, Copyright Maithreyi Nandakumar ©2016

Underground by Carolyn Stubbs – Original short story, also a supernatural film of the same name directed by Markus Etter Photograph, Copyright Joe Beasant © 2016

Author Biographies

Eileen Elsey aka D A Allen (Dec'd)

Writing as D A Allen, Eileen Elsey was a former scriptwriter, reporter and academic, who discovered the joys of short story writing through the Bristol Fiction Writers' Group, sadly she never finished her historical novel based on the Bristol Riots. She had several stories included in A Dark Imagined Bristol, the first anthology from the Bristol Fiction Writers Group.

Allen came to Bristol from London some years ago, and found the city intriguing both in history and as a location.

Elizabeth Ann 'Liz' Ascott (Dec'd)

Liz Ascott completed public and private art commissions in England, Scotland, Spain, France & the USA.

Her short stories and illustrations were nurtured in south Bristol, where the mists of autumn rise and the fungal rings close in on those foolish enough to stumble through its dark, dank streets and hidden parks.

Liz had several stories published in A Dark Imagined Bristol, the first anthology from The Bristol Fiction Writers Group

Joe Beasant

Joe Beasant is a professional photographer, creative woodworker and currently working on a historical novel. His photographic skills are used to document the fast paced national sport of Horseboarding UK, yet on the flip side he will capture the atmosphere of an early morning mist or the quiet beauty of a still life subject, just as an artist might do. He also paints.

A A Abbott

Having lived in London and Birmingham, Abbott now lives in a garden square in Bristol. Working peripherally in the corporate world she uses her experiences to fire gripping thrillers and sharply observed short stories.

Find her on Facebook and Twitter @AAAbbottStories

Judy Darley

Judy Darley is a fiction writer, poet and journalist. Her work has been published by literary magazines, in anthologies and in her short story collection *Remember Me To The Bees*. She's read her short fiction on BBC radio, as well as in cafés, caves, an artist's studio and in a disused church. Judy blogs about art and other things at www.skylightrain.com, and tweets @JudyDarley.

J E Hagan

For many years the only stories J E told were to avoid cross country running at school, in fact school, generally. A family and three businesses later she returned to her studies with an Open University degree, during which she got the bug for fiction writing. She has had flash fiction published on t'internet, as Peter Kay calls it, and taken part in flash fiction gigs.

Richard M S Kemp

Back from the US and residing in England, Richard M S Kemp is a writer and journalist. He writes creative fiction and is founder of online music magazine Kemptation www.Kemptation.com

Tim Kindberg

Tim Kindberg works in digital media as a researcher, artist and developer, and writes in his spare time. He has self-published a YA novel, Shadows of Marrakech, and is working on two further novels. He has had poems and short stories published. Until recently he was a director and occasional editor of Magma poetry magazine. More about him at www.champignon.net and @timkindberg.

Nigel Lapworth

For Nigel writing is both a relaxing hobby and part time obsession. He likes to write about quirky subjects – some would say disparate, but you can usually rely on a twist, a laugh or something to make the hairs rise on your neck. He is also a well-known local musician and has even been accused of occasionally teaching the piano.

Maithreyi Nandakumar

Maithreyi Nandakumar writes fiction and is a journalist working in print and sound. Her short-stories have been published in anthologies (First Prize, Bristol Tales), broadcast on World Service and Radio Bristol, online (Toasted Cheese, Over the Red Line) and made the last 16 for BBC Opening Lines 2014. Her completed novel 'Stirring the Pot,' for which she received a generous grant from the Arts Council (Southwest), is awaiting fame and fortune.

Suzanna Stanbury

Suzanna has been writing since childhood. She writes children's books, novels, and short stories, publishing online on Kindle, Barnes and Noble and Smashwords, and in paperback form on Lulu.com. Suzanna is the administrator and an active member of the Bristol Fiction Writers' Group. She performs at spoken word events, schools and children's groups.

Website: www.snubtry.weebly.com

YouTube:

https://www.youtube.com/channel/UCftDKzGqFskxeuOy Y1uvEBQ

Carolyn Stubbs

Carolyn Stubbs is a published writer of fiction and non-fiction who wrote the script for the film *'Underground'*. She is also an award winning artist with work exhibited throughout the UK, New York and held in private collections. Her sculpted paper technique, often used to depict wildlife, was included in *'State of the Art'* art book. More information can be found on www.carolynstubbs.co.uk

Lightning Source UK Ltd.
Milton Keynes UK
UKOW05f0403270417
300002UK00001B/112/P